EARL OF GRAYSON

AMANDA MARIEL

BROOK RIDGE PRESS

Damien Archer, the Earl of Grayson, reclined on a leather armchair with a glass of brandy firmly in hand. The Wicked Earls' Club bustled with patrons, and Damien was pleased to be among them. Over the years, the club had become a second home to him. He spent numerous hours within the safety of its walls gambling and partaking of women and booze. He did not want to imagine what life would be like without his club.

"I cannot believe another of us has willingly handed over his key." Damien shook his head. It seemed that one earl after another had disappeared from within these walls over the last few months.

Benton, who sat opposite Damien, swirled the

liquor in his tumbler. "Who do you suppose will be next?"

"So long as it's not me, I don't bloody care." Davenport took a swig of his whiskey and stretched his legs out in front of him as he reclined in the chair across from Damien.

Far too many of their fellow earls had left the club as of late—Sussex, Westcliff, and Basingstoke among them. Each had become love-bitten and then chose to marry. The consequence being that they had to turn in their pins and keys and leave the club —forever.

Damien would never make such a choice. "I second, Davenport," Damien said. "In fact, if I should ever be so stupid as to consider it, please take me out into the woods and shoot me at once."

Benton's eyes rounded for a moment before he began to chuckle. "You would not want us to carry out that wish if you actually fell in love."

"The hell I wouldn't!" Damien drained his tumbler and then signaled for a refill.

"What do you know of love?" Davenport appraised Benton.

"Only that it makes a man lose all sense." Benton glanced at the large floor-to-ceiling window. "It is hard to believe that any skirt could wreak such havoc, and yet we've seen it time and again."

Damien shook his head and stood. "Far too often for my comfort."

"Where are you off to?" Davenport asked, one eyebrow arched.

"Wouldn't you like to know?" Damien walked away, leaving them to wonder. He could have told them he was heading for home, but why disappoint them? Surely they expected something far different, like a house of ill repute, a mistress, or a gaming hell. The truth was, he would rather be off to engage in something wild and reckless if he weren't so bloody tired.

He stifled a yawn as he exited the Wicked Earls' Club. He'd spent the previous evening carousing at his usual haunts with Edgemore. Then, after a few hours of sleep, he'd ventured to the club. Now he found himself in need of more rest. Perhaps once he'd had a nap, he would find some more fun to partake in.

After giving his driver orders, Damien settled against the plush seat of his carriage and allowed his eyes to close. Before long the carriage jostled and turned into the long drive of his Mayfair mansion.

Sitting up straight, he adjusted his coat as the conveyance came to a stop.

He wasted no time stepping down from the carriage intent on reaching his front door, and more importantly, his bed. Halfway across the drive, the pounding of hooves drew his attention. Damien glanced up the gravel drive, releasing a heavy sigh.

Two women raced toward him mounted on white horses.

Who the devil were they, and what did they want?

Damien peered at the riders, attempting to make out their features. He focused on the one in front. When she came into view, all of the air left his lungs as if someone had punched him in the gut. He forgot all about her companion as disbelief and shock gripped him—shaking him to the core.

Lady Charlotte Lawson—pale blond curls bouncing as her small frame sat proudly upon her mount. He'd wager her icy blue eyes sparkled with merriment, though he could not see them to be sure. Of all the woman who could have been racing up his drive, it was her—his Charlotte.

No, not anymore. She hadn't been his in years. Why had she come? Did he even care?

Charlotte pulled up on the reins, slowing her

mount before bringing the horse to a stop. "I had so hoped to find you here." She gave a charming smile, eyes sparkling just as he'd imagined they would be.

She shifted in the saddle, pinning him beneath her stare. "Don't just stand there, Damien. Do come help me down. I must speak with you at once."

Momentarily incapable of words or actions, he risked a glance at the other rider. Charlotte's sister Lady Elizabeth, or rather, Lady Oxford since she'd wed, had pulled rein several yards behind Charlotte.

"Well," Charlotte said, her voice laced with impatience.

Damien drew in a breath as he stepped closer, his gaze holding hers. "Why are you here?"

"Help me out of this saddle, and then I will be glad to enlighten you." She impatiently dropped the reins, allowing them to hang across the horse's shoulder. "Or am I to jump down on my own?"

How many years had passed since he'd last spoken with her? Ten? Twelve? He had seen her about the *ton;* at balls, musicals, and other events on occasion, but he had not spoken with her—not one word since the day he'd set her free.

It had been for the best back then—it still was. "I have no need to hear you out." Damien pivoted and began strolling toward the shelter of his home.

"Wait. This is important," Charlotte called after him.

A moment later the sound of her half boots racing across his drive assaulted his ears. Bloody hell. Why would she not go away? Before he could react, she reached out and grabbed his arm.

"I will not allow you to walk away from me. Not this time, Damien." Determination radiated from within her.

He held her gaze, all fire and fury, making the icy-blue of her eyes crackle. "It is a tad late for anger now. Wouldn't you say?" He pulled his arm free from her grasp. "Go home, Charlotte."

"I cannot. Leastwise not until after you have granted me an audience."

As she spoke, desperation seeped into her gaze. Perhaps he had her all wrong. Maybe this had nothing to do with their past. Could she be in some sort of trouble? Damien crossed his arms over his chest and released a huff of breath. "Very well. Start talking."

"Might we go inside first?" Charlotte glanced at the large oak door Damien's servant now held open. "It is a delicate matter."

"Delicate?" He arched one brow as he studied her.

"Indeed." Her cheeks flushed, but she held her ground.

Good God, had she gone and gotten herself with child? He swept his gaze over the familiar curves of her body. He'd kill the bastard, see him quartered and dragged through the streets. Damien took hold of Charlotte's elbow and led her into the house, down the hall, and into his receiving room.

He shut the door behind them before turning to her. "Who did this to you?"

"Wha...what?" Her eyes rounded.

"Who is the bloody libertine that took advantage of you? I will see him punished." Damien leaned closer, his tone deadly. "He will suffer, I promise you."

Charlotte notched her chin. "The only man who has ever taken advantage of me...is you."

Damien released her elbow and strolled across the room. Thank goodness he'd been wrong. The very thought of anyone ruining her set his blood to boiling. It was for that very reason he'd turned away from her all those years ago.

Charlotte was no light skirt—she was a true, pure lady in need of a husband. He would never marry, and therefore, he would never be deserving of her.

"Tell me, Damien, have you suffered?" Her voice drifted across the space.

He ignored the stab of guilt and the way his heartbeat seemed to skip at her words. "Dispense with the games, Charlotte." Reaching the fireplace, he turned back to her. "Tell me, why the devil have you come?"

Charlotte reached up, fidgeting with the trim adorning her riding habit's bodice. "I want you to teach me how to seduce a man."

He swallowed hard, bringing his attention back to her face. "Come again?"

She could not possibly have asked him what he thought she did. It was unconscionable. Improper. Not at all like the Charlotte he'd known.

Certainly not the type of request a well-bred lady should make. He narrowed his gaze on her as he rolled the words around his mind.

"I can think of no one better suited to the task than you. After all, you are a renowned rakehell." She took a few slow strides toward him. "Furthermore, I know how persuasive your skills can be."

This must be some sort of ploy. He could fathom no other explanation. "You cannot be serious, Charlotte."

"I assure you I am." She notched her chin, defiance etched on her face.

Damien came to stand in front of her, his gaze burning into hers. "Why?"

"I wish to charm gentlemen, of course." She averted her gaze to the window and sighed.

"You are not the type." Damien ground out the words. The mere thought of any man touching her, bedding her, made him want to strangle someone.

Her attention returned to him. "I most certainly am."

No, she was not—never had been. Not that she was a prude. He could have easily taken her virtue all those years ago. She'd offered herself to him, been willing to give him every part of her. She had been in love with him. Planned a future with him as her husband.

He shook his head. "That is why you have brought a chaperone along?"

"She is here to make sure you do not take your lessons too far. A safety measure of sorts." Charlotte glanced back out the window to where her sister remained in the drive, still on her mount. "You see, I have no wish to be ruined. I only want to learn how to tempt a man, not bed one."

Her tone cut through him as her words trailed

off. She did not trust him and harbored anger over the past. Still, she had come to him for help. He closed his eyes while rubbing his forehead between his thumb and fingers. "Should I agree, what do you hope to accomplish with your new knowledge?

Charlotte smiled at him. "Marriage."

He laughed. "I am not the sort."

"You are not my mark. The *ton* is full of well-suited gentlemen. I hope to gain the interest and affection of one of them before I become an irrevocable spinster. And besides, you owe me."

"Do I?" His grin faltered.

"Indeed, you do. I gave you my heart all those years ago. I spent my most marriageable years pining for you, waiting for you to come back to me. Do you know what they called me?" She did not wait for him to answer before continuing on. "The unattainable debutante."

"I will not apologize," Damien said. He had loved her enough to leave her chaste. She would not make him feel bad for his decision; for he knew that he'd done what was best for them both.

"By the time I accepted that you would not be coming back to me, I'd earned a reputation for turning suitors away, and the unattainable debutante I have stayed ever since. Now I am nearing nine and twenty with no prospects." Her shoulders slumped. "It is not my wish to spend my life alone."

How he wanted to take her in his arms and kiss her at this very moment. The image of her soft, creamy skin bared for him flashed to the front of his mind and he stepped closer, stopping himself just short of taking her into his embrace.

Bloody hell, spending time with her would damn near kill him, but how could he refuse? He did *owe* her. "Stop pouting, you win."

A bright smile lit her face. "Thank you, Damien, thank you, thank you, thank you." She embraced him, pressing her breasts against his chest. "When shall we begin?"

Damien took her arms from around him and stepped back. He could not trust himself so close to her. "Tonight, at the Brighton Ball. I had not planned to attend, but since you will be among the guests, I will come and observe your interactions. Then I can determine how best to aid you in your endeavor."

She angled her head, her eyes narrowing. "I already told you how to help. I need to learn how to seduce a man."

Good lord, he wished she would stop saying that. Every time her sweet mouth formed the words, he wanted to plunder her. Shaking his head, he said,

"Seduction would only lead you to ruin. What you need to do is charm the *ton's* gentlemen, capture their interest, and make it known that you are available for marriage."

She darted her tongue out, wetting her lips. "Very well, I will see you this evening."

Damien did his best to ignore the discomfort of his swollen manhood pressing against his trousers as she turned to take her leave of the room. How could she not already know the effect she had on a man? It was all he could do to keep from ravishing her.

Charlotte possessed great beauty, a true Diamond of the first water. Her light coloring, small frame, and feminine curves were what first drew him to her. But she possessed wit and charm as well as a tender soul. Those attributes had nearly stolen his heart.

Could he still be susceptible to her charms? Did he place them both in danger by agreeing to her scheme?

Bloody hell, he released a huff of breath and reached for his brandy decanter.

The sooner he got her safely wed, the better.

CHAPTER 2

As Charlotte made her way from Damien's parlor, her mind flashed back to their last clandestine meeting. She could still feel his arms wrapped around her, still smell his masculine scent, and would never be able to forget the cold, haunted look in his gaze as he'd turned her away.

That night, eleven years ago, she'd snuck out of a ball to meet him in private. Trepidation had not tingled against her spine, neither had nerves set her on edge. Rather, excitement for the future had filled her along with a powerful longing to be with the man she loved.

She had been determined to give herself to Damien—body and soul. There had been no reason to wait since she was quite certain he would be offering for her soon. How could he not? They spent every moment they could together and took every opportunity to be alone, often sneaking off to meet in dark corners.

When she had entered the conservatory, she'd run into his arms. Damien pulled her close, nuzzling his face against her upswept hair.

"I must speak with you in all seriousness, Charlotte." His long-ago words echoed back to her.

Charlotte had tipped her chin up to gaze at him. "I have something to tell you as well." She dropped kisses on his neck before nuzzling her face into his warm flesh and murmuring against him, "I love you, Damien. I do not want to wait any longer. Make love to me."

When she'd tipped her chin up to gaze into his eyes, he'd brought his mouth to hers in a bruising kiss. Her insides had ignited in a flurry of passion as she'd pressed against him. When they finally parted she'd clung to him, her heart bursting with love, anticipation prickling at her as she awaited his declaration of love—his proposal of marriage.

Instead, he stated his intention never to marry—shattering her heart.

As the memory faded from her mind, the pain stung her as though minutes rather than years had lapsed. Perhaps it was being in his embrace again that had reopened the old wound. She should never have hugged him, no matter how grateful she was for his assistance.

But then, it could be not knowing why he'd acted as he had that bothered her. She'd received no explanation—no closure.

That long-ago night when he'd shattered her dreams, he'd given her no reason for his rejection, simply said they were not to be then left her standing alone in the conservatory, staring after him with kiss-swollen lips and broken dreams.

She gathered her skirt in her hand as she descended the steps of his porch. As badly as she wished to run, she would maintain her composure. She had to, Elizabeth was watching, and for all she knew, Damien was too.

In the years since their parting, Charlotte had spent countless hours searching the gossip columns for any news of him, and even more hours crying into her pillows. She had eventually hardened her heart, turning all of her love to hatred. The last thing she had expected when she came to him this afternoon was to feel those old hurts afresh. She'd be damned if she allowed anyone else to discover how he had affected her.

God's bones, after what he'd done to her, she should not have any passionate feelings toward him —let alone tender ones. What the devil was wrong with her?

Charlotte marched across his drive toward her horse, clutching the skirt of her riding habit so hard that her knuckles turned white. Perhaps enlisting his help had been a mistake. Regardless, she could think of no other means to achieve her end. She'd set her course in motion and she meant to follow it through. Where Damien was concerned, she would have to keep an emotional distance in order to protect herself, but he was still best suited to help her.

With the aid of a footman, she swung into her saddle. Hazarding a glance at her sister, she took the reins and set her horse into a canter. The breeze created by her fast pace calmed her as she guided her horse out of the gravel drive.

"Must we ride at such a breakneck pace?" Elizabeth yelled, glancing at Charlotte.

Rather than giving an answer, Charlotte simply pushed her mount faster.

Elizabeth caught up, then glared at at Charlotte. "Do slow down and tell me how things went with Lord Grayson."

"Let us return home first, lest someone see us

and gossip about our outing." She dismissed her sister, focusing her attention on the road ahead.

Charlotte was not ready to discuss the success of her meeting yet, for fear that Elizabeth would see through to her angst. Elizabeth had warned her that seeing Damien could stir up old emotions, but Charlotte had insisted that no love remained. She wasn't ready to bask in her sister's gloating. As it were, they would be home too soon for Charlotte's liking.

After gaining some distance from Damien, Charlotte slowed her horse's pace, and they rode the remaining distance in companionable silence. Elizabeth followed Charlotte from the stables and into their home before speaking again.

"Now will you tell what happened at Lord Grayson's?" Elizabeth followed Charlotte up the stairs. "Or am I to guess?"

"I asked him to help and he agreed." Reaching the top of the grand staircase, Charlotte turned down the corridor that led to her rooms. She hoped Elizabeth would go her own way without added conversation. Clearly, she was not to be so lucky considering her sister had followed her up the stairs.

"What marvelous news indeed! Your hasty retreat made me fear that he'd refused."

Charlotte entered her bedchamber with Elizabeth close behind. Turning to her sister, she said, "I intend to have a bath and perhaps a nap before the ball." It should have been enough to send Elizabeth on her way, but Charlotte was not to gain an easy escape.

She sighed when her sister lowered herself into an armchair. "Do you not have preparations to make for the ball? Surely your husband expects you home soon."

"Never mind all of that." Elizabeth removed her gloves and laid them in her lap. "I want to hear how Lord Grayson plans to aid you."

Charlotte tossed her bonnet onto the bed, then strolled across the room and rang for her maid. While her back was to Elizabeth, she said, "He plans to attend tonight's ball and observe my interactions."

"And then what?" Elizabeth asked.

Charlotte turned to her sister. "Then he will determine how best to help me."

"You were with him for an absurd amount of time. What took so long?" Elizabeth stared at her through suspicious blue eyes. "Did he force you to beg? Or worse, try to take liberties with you?"

Charlotte smoothed her skirt. "No...not exactly." She glanced at the window. How much did she dare tell Elizabeth? She brought her attention back to her sister. "It was worse than all that. He made me explain my motivation and my reason for enlisting him to help."

Elizabeth's eyes softened, and she came to stand beside Charlotte. "Are you quite certain you wish to go through with this scheme? I do not want to see you hurt. I'm certain you could find a suitable match without Lord Grayson's interference."

Elizabeth had stood by Charlotte through her heartbreak all those years ago and knew all too well what Charlotte had gone through. She did not blame her sister for harboring concerns now. In truth, Charlotte fretted as well. "I am determined to find a husband."

"I am well aware, dear." Elizabeth wrapped her arm around Charlotte's shoulders. "But are you sure that you want Lord Grayson's help with the matter?"

"There is no one better suited to the task." Charlotte gave a bright smile. She hoped it appeared cheery, rather than one of those frightful forced ones. "Now do take your leave so that I may prepare for the ball. After all, it does promise to be an important night."

Elizabeth gave Charlotte a slight squeeze before she released her. "I will see you this evening."

Indeed, Charlotte would see a great many people

—including Damien. Her traitorous heart sped up at the thought as she watched Elizabeth depart. Would Damien dance with her? Would he think her stunning in her new ball gown?

She heaved a sigh, shaking her head at the foolish pondering. He'd broken her heart. She didn't give a fig what he did or thought now, just so long as he helped her.

CHAPTER 3

*D*amien watched as Charlotte sat along the edge of the room with the other wallflowers and spinsters. She'd been there all night, rooted as firmly to her chair as the ferns decorating the ballroom were to their pots. It was no wonder she lacked suitors when she did not so much as try to interact. No curious gazes, no welcoming smiles, nothing at all to indicate a willingness to mingle with the other guests.

What had happened to the vivacious beauty he had once courted? She cut a lovely image in her pale ball gown, but gone were the brilliant smiles and sparkling eyes. Charlotte used to light up the ballroom with her brilliant smiles and giddy laughter. Now her light seemed to have burnt out as she sat there looking as dull as an unlit room. It was no wonder the *ton's* gentlemen did not approach her. Between her bored expression and stiff posture, she looked rather stern—not at all welcoming despite being the most attractive lady present.

Having seen enough, Damien strolled across the expanse of the candlelit room. He would have to get her out of that chair if he were ever to help her succeed in finding a husband. He made his way through the crush, weaving in and out of clusters of people and potted ferns, then grabbed two flutes of champagne from a servant before approaching Charlotte.

When he reached the thrall of wallflowers, he thrust one of the flutes into Charlotte's hand. "Drink this."

Her pale blue eyes grew wide. "I do not want to."

He tipped his flute against his lips and drained the champagne from it in one long draw before pinning her with his gaze. "Drink it."

Charlotte stared back at him for a moment then did as he had, draining the contents of the flute in one long drink. Holding the glass back out to him, she said, "Are you happy now?"

"No." He reached out taking her hand then

pulled her from the chair. "You cannot sit here all night and hope to garner any attention."

"What would you have me do when no one has signed my dance card?" she protested as he led her away from the wall. "It is not as if I can force them to."

"I don't blame them." Damien stopped on the dance floor and pulled her into his arms.

Charlotte peered up at him. "What is that supposed to mean?"

"You have not moved from that chair all night."

"I do not recall you as being daft."

"And I do not remember you as a cold marble statue." Damien twirled her then brought her back into his arms as he led them through the steps of the dance. "You cannot expect gentlemen to approach you when you do nothing to invite their attention."

Charlotte pressed her eyes closed. When she opened them again, she stared directly into his. "What would you have me do?"

"To start with, you could smile." Damien had always adored her smile. The way her full pink lips parted revealing her perfect pearl-white teeth while the apples of her cheeks rose and rounded had always drawn him in. His gaze settled on her plump lips and he found himself wishing he could taste them once more. Pushing the thought into the shadows of his mind, he said, "Go on, smile for me."

She gave a half-hearted grin.

"Brighter."

Her lips parted, the corners of her mouth pulling up.

"Yes, like that." He twirled her once more, then brought her back into his arms. "Next, you must not sit with the wallflowers."

"Then what do you suggest I do?"

"Take a turn about the room, go onto the veranda for a bit of fresh air, or lurk around the refreshment table. For heaven's sake, do anything other than what you have been."

She nibbled at her lower lip, the light in her eyes dimming. "I will endeavor to try."

His heart hitched at the knowledge he had hurt her. Still, if he were going to help her, he had to be honest. Somehow, he had to coax the old Charlotte back to the surface. "What happened to you? These things used to be second nature for you."

She did not answer—not with words at any rate, but the faraway look in her crystal blue eyes spoke volumes. He had done more than break her heart—he'd destroyed her confidence. Damien's heart grew heavy. The last thing he had ever wanted to do was hurt her, and until this moment he hadn't even realized how much he had.

What a blackguard he'd been—was still being. No more. He would do whatever he had to in order to restore her confidence and vivacity.

"Charlotte." His voice came out barely louder than a whisper.

She brought her attention back to him, peering up tentatively through her thick veil of eyelashes.

"You are a beautiful woman, and as I recall, quite capable of being charming and witty when you choose to be. You need only show it and you will have more suitors than you will know what to do with."

She laughed, a genuine smile overcoming her. "That was very kind of you to say."

"I meant every word." The quartet struck the final notes of the dance, and Damien swept Charlotte from the dance floor then led her to where her sister stood. He bowed. "Good evening, Lady Oxford," he greeted.

"I see you have located my sister, Lord Grayson. I trust you enjoyed your dance." Elizabeth waved her silk fan.

"Indeed, and now I am returning her to you."

Before Charlotte could release his arm and step away he leaned close and whispered, "Stay here."

She nodded, then turned to her sister as he took his leave of them. Now that he had her away from that bloody chair, he had to ensure that she did not return to it. There was one way to make certain she remained amongst the crush rather than sequestered in a corner.

Damien turned from the sisters with a plan in mind and searched the room for his intended helper. Spotting the Duchess of Goodwin, he strolled across the ballroom.

"Your Grace." He gave a roguish grin, dropping into a bow.

The Duchess grinned, her eyes dancing. "Whatever are you doing here?"

"Enjoying the ball, of course."

"You never attend these sorts of things without good cause. Do tell me what you are about." She gave a lopsided grin before sipping her champagne.

"I never could fool you." He granted her another charming grin. He'd not reveal his reason for attending. The duchess was a renowned gossip, a fact he intended to use to his advantage—not the other way around. "I hear tell that the unattainable debutante is seeking a husband."

"Is that so?" Her Grace's gaze swept across the room to where Charlotte stood beside Lady Oxford. "How is it that I am only now hearing of this?"

"Truly?" He raised a brow in mock surprise. "You are normally among the first to hear such tidbits."

"Be that as it may, I shall not be the last." She playfully smacked her fan against his arm. "Excuse me."

He bowed, then turned his attention back to Charlotte as the duchess made her way toward a pack of gossips. By night's end, everyone who was anyone in London would know of Charlotte's desire to wed. Having done all he could, for now, Damien returned to Charlotte's side. "A word, my lady."

She took his proffered arm and allowed him to lead her around the perimeter of the ballroom. The instant she touched him, his blood heated—white-hot desire ripping through him.

Dammit, but the woman still had a hold on him. Swallowing hard, Damien glanced at her. "I am going to take my leave. I have seen enough for one night. You are to remain standing and keep smiling. Before long, your dance card is going to fill up."

"How can you be so sure?"

He led her back toward Lady Oxford. "Trust me...it will."

"Won't you stay so that you might give me more guidance?" She stared at him with pleading eyes.

"You do not need any more of my help. Simply accept the dances and be yourself."

"What if my card remains empty?"

"I promise it will not." He deposited her back with her sister, then took his leave before she could press him further. The ballroom had become stifling. He tugged at his cravat which presently threatened to cut off his air supply. Bloody hell, he was still far too attracted to Charlotte.

Quickening his pace, Damien turned into the hall then wasted no time ordering his carriage brought round. He could not stand the idea of paying witness to all of the attention Charlotte was about to receive. He wanted—no needed to leave at once.

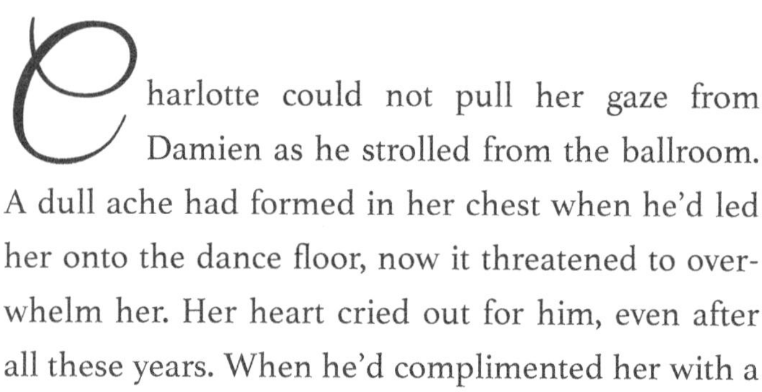

harlotte could not pull her gaze from Damien as he strolled from the ballroom. A dull ache had formed in her chest when he'd led her onto the dance floor, now it threatened to over-whelm her. Her heart cried out for him, even after all these years. When he'd complimented her with a shower of pretty words as he held her close, she'd been compelled to kiss him. Then she'd made a perfect cake of herself by laughing instead.

What the devil was wrong with her? She squeezed her eyes shut and shook her head. On second thought, what the devil was wrong with him? Why had he spoken to her in such a way? And with such conviction, too. She opened her eyes seeking him out once more.

Had he truly meant what he'd said? He'd called her beautiful, charming, and witty. Her stomach fluttered at the memory. Try as she may to suppress her feelings for him, a piece of her heart would always belong to the scoundrel. Even now, she wanted nothing more than to be back in his warm, strong arms.

"Ow!" Charlotte jerked to look at Elizabeth who had just whacked her with her fan. She rubbed arm just below her shoulder as she peered at her sister. "What was that for?"

"You have to stop mooning over Lord Grayson." Elizabeth pointed her fan at Charlotte as she spoke. "He is not for you."

"I'm not mooning over anyone. Least of all him." Even as she said it, Charlotte knew she was fibbing. Judging by the peer Elizabeth leveled on her, she wasn't buying Charlotte's words either. Charlotte gave a slight grin. "I was simply watching him go."

"It's for the best." Elizabeth reached out and patted Charlotte's shoulder. "You will see in time."

Charlotte glanced across the ballroom, hoping to catch one more glimpse of Damien. Her heart hitched, he was gone. She turned her attention back to Elizabeth. "Yes, of course."

"You haven't any time to waste on Lord Grayson at any rate." Elizabeth pointed her offending fan at a group of lords who presently strolled in their direction. "It seems your dance card is about to fill in."

Charlotte pasted what she hoped was an inviting smile on her lips. This was what she'd wanted. The very thing she'd asked Damien to help her with. She pushed all thought of him back into the shadows of her mind and turned her attention to the approaching gentlemen.

CHAPTER 4

"Another one?" Charlotte said with delight as she instructed her maid to place the bouquet of pink roses on her side table. Damien had been correct when he'd told her that her dance card would soon be full. Elizabeth had been right as well and delighted in Charlotte's newfound popularity. Charlotte had danced every set, not leaving the ball until after three in the morning. She'd left weary and with sore feet, but she'd not have wished it any other way.

And now—well, this morning her home looked more like a greenhouse than a London townhouse. It could hardly contain all of the flowers she'd received. Roses in every shade, poppies, lilies, orchids, and lilacs spread their sweet perfume throughout the space. Not to mention the more than a dozen invitations and callers she'd entertained today. What a marvelous change from the days prior. Hope swelled within her, for surely she would find a suitable husband soon.

How had Damien pulled it off? She'd gone from being the unattainable debutante to the most sought-after lady in London, leastwise that is what all of the attention made her feel like. She sniffed the bouquet of pink lilies on her side table. How would she choose from among the many suitors?

She did not hope to find love—she'd already done that years ago and feared her heart would always be with Damien. She doubted she could ever love another. She resigned herself to settle for a man whom she could care for, one who cared for her as well. A man who would treat her well and provide a good home. And though doubtful, perhaps given enough time—just maybe—love would blossom between her and her chosen husband.

At the least, she wished for a man who would be her companion, partner, friend, and lover. For that, the gentleman she chose would have to have similar interests and a genuine wish to wed her. He did not have to be titled or even wealthy, but he did have to want her for herself and the future she would bring.

Charlotte released a deep breath. She did not know the first thing about determining a man's genuine interest. If she did, Damien never would have fooled her as he had.

Oh, Damien. Yes, he would be able to tell her how to sort out the men who were truly enamored with her from those seeking her dowry or an elevated status, or just as bad, a broodmare to provide his heir then wither in loneliness. A shiver coursed through her. She would go to him and ask for more guidance.

You no longer need my help. His words echoed through her mind and her heart hitched. He was mistaken; she very much needed his guidance and tutelage. Even once she determined which men were genuine, she would still need to charm her chosen husband. Seduce him into an offer, into wanting to spend his life with her.

However, given Damien's words, perhaps a letter would serve her better than appearing on his doorstep as she had no wish to incite his anger.

Charlotte sat down at her carved cherry wood writing desk and drew a piece of parchment from the drawer before setting it on the hard surface and taking up her quill. She would write to Damien at once to request his ongoing assistance as well as his attendance at the Gilford musical this evening.

D,

You are mistaken to assume that I no longer need your assistance. As it were, I am as lost as ever. How am I to determine which of my suitors truly cares for me? Do attend the Gilford musical this evening so that you might help me in my endeavor--as you promised you would.

Sincerely,

C

She folded the parchment, sealed it, and then gave it to a footman with instructions to deliver it at once. There was nothing left for her to do other than prepare herself for the evening's entertainments— and hope Damien would acquiesce to her request.

Charlotte arrived at the Gilford's musical at thirty minutes past. The performance would soon begin, and Damien had yet to appear. Every time someone entered her attention turned to the door as she gazed at the newcomers, hoping to find him.

She nibbled her lower lip as Lord Demount led her around the room. She really ought to be paying the gentleman more attention. She'd danced with him at the Brighton ball and he'd sent her a lovely bouquet the next morning before coming to call. The gentleman was handsome with his aristocratic features, though his jaw was not near as chiseled as Damien's—nor were his eyes as captivating, nor his body as well-formed...

Charlotte sighed. She should not compare her suitors to Damien. It was not fair to anyone—least of all her. No man would ever come close to him as far as she was concerned. She ought to be thankful for that, for it meant that none of them could break her heart. She smiled at Lord Demount. "Tell me, what is your favorite sweet-treat?"

"I do not care for sweet foods, my lady" he replied without animation.

Surely they had something in common. She'd try again. "Have you been to the opera of late?"

"Gads no. The opera does naught but make my headache."

Charlotte forced a smile. "How about horses, Lord Demount. Have you a favorite equestrian activity?"

"I fear not. I have no use for the beasts other than pulling my carriage." He laughed.

Charlotte cringed inwardly. She found nothing humorous about his answer. Further, she could not abide a gentleman who did not care for horses. After all, she was an avid horsewoman. She supposed

Lord Demount could be taken off her list of potential suitors.

Lord Demount returned her to her mother and they took their seats as the musical began. Charlotte would do her best to avoid the man's company in the future. She swept her gaze over the room hoping to catch sight of Damien before turning her attention to the front of the room. The devil had ignored her request, and she didn't know whether to be upset or relieved.

Why agree to help her if he only intended to stir up a batch of potential suitors and then abandon her without further care? He'd proven in short order that he remained the same cold-hearted rogue he'd been eleven years ago. Devil take him, she didn't give a fig if he helped or not.

She focused her attention on the Gilford's oldest daughter, who was playing the pianoforte. The girl worked the ivory keys with mastery, filling the room with a haunting tune. Charlotte let herself drift along with the music, all thoughts fleeing her mind.

"You look lovely."

She jumped, startled at first by the low, smooth voice, and then by the warmth of someone breathing so near to her ear and neck. Her heart pounding, she turned and locked gazes with Damien. A thrill shot through her at his nearness as she took in the fine cut of his black coat and perfectly tied white cravat, his broad shoulders, and dark sparkling eyes. Mercy, but he was the most handsome man she'd ever beheld.

He settled into the chair beside her and turned a lazy, roguish grin, in her direction. His cocoa-colored eyes alight with mischief. Charlotte swept her gaze over him from his black hair to his buff breeches and shining hessian boots, his white cravat standing out in deep contrast to the rest of his attire.

Her cheeks warmed as she peered at him. "You startled me."

"I should do so more often." He leaned closer stroking his finger across her burning cheek. "You are adorable when caught unawares. Even more so when you blush."

Her entire body heated at his compliment, his touch. Her stomach fluttered and the feminine spot between her thighs began to throb. The devil if he did not still get to her, even after all these years. She wished she could sink through the floorboards and disappear, for surely he noticed her reaction—realized that she still desired him. His widening smile was all the proof she required.

"Hush, and do watch the musical." Charlotte

turned her attention back to the front of the room. Though she could no longer see Damien, she could feel his eyes on her. The heat he'd started in her threatened to turn her to cinders. Every inch of her skin tingled and begged for more of his caresses.

How she wished to gaze at him, to touch him back, though she knew it would only lead to disaster. She swallowed hard, pushing her thoughts away and trying to focus on the music.

Charlotte spent the remainder of the show attempting to ignore Damien's nearness. When the music ended, at last, she flipped open her fan and began cooling her still burning cheeks.

"Perhaps a spot of fresh air would help, my lady," Damien said.

Charlotte turned her head toward him. She should absolutely not allow him to escort her anywhere, but she did need to speak to him. "Indeed," She said, then looked to her mother. "Mama, might I take a turn around the garden with Lord Grayson?"

Mother smiled, rising from her chair, and Charlotte feared she may wish to join them. Pray no, for if she did Charlotte would not be able to speak to him about her gentlemen callers. She forced a grin and waited with bated breath for Mother's reply.

"Very well, darling. I will meet you back here after the break." Mother strolled toward the center aisle, leaving Charlotte in Damien's care.

He stood and held out his hand to assist her. "Allow me."

Charlotte accepted his arm and he swept her from the room. Within minutes, he had led her down a shaded garden path. Though she did not wish to be vulgar, she found it preferable to spending too much time in his company. Therefore, she skipped small talk and polite topics in order to get straight to the heart of her summons before she did something foolish. "How am I to know which of my many suitors are truly interested in me?"

"It is not like you to skirt propriety as you are. First coming to my home, and now blurting out inappropriate questions." He gave a teasing grin. "Your Mother would be aghast."

"Do not jest. This is serious. I do not want to make another mistake." His attention drifted from her and she knew he'd taken her meaning. Damien had crushed her, ruined her dreams, destroyed her faith in love—she'd not submit herself to such pain again. Not willingly.

"I am sorry, Charlotte. It was never my intention

to hurt you." He rubbed small circles on her gloved hand where it rested on his coat sleeve.

His attentions were too much. She'd surely crumble if he continued on with his apologies and caring glances. She lifted her chin. "Never mind the past. Tell me your thoughts on Lord Gartner?"

"He's no good." Damien shook his head firmly.

"Why not?" Charlotte asked.

"He is not for you." Damien led her down a path lined with hedges that split off to the right. "He drinks too much and too often."

"Very well." She slanted her gaze toward him. "What of Lord Merryweather?"

"He's far too lazy."

Lord Gartner and Lord Merryweather were at the top of her list of potential husbands. No more, she supposed. Charlotte inhaled the sweet scent of the hyacinths they were strolling past. Surely there were worthy gentlemen among her callers. She glanced again at Damien and asked, "Lord Rutherford, Lord Barton, or Mr. Larkford?"

"No, no, and certainly not," Damien said, his tone leaving no room for argument.

Charlotte could not help but laugh. It seemed he would find fault with every man she mentioned.

How absurd. "Pray, tell me what issue you take with those gentlemen?"

"Rutherford is in need of a wealthy bride. Barton gambles into the wee morning hours, sometimes not stopping for days. And as for Larkford...he has a terrible sense of fashion. The man's cravats are never neatly tied, and last week he wore an orange coat."

Charlotte laughed again at the absurdity of Damien's objections to Mr. Larkford. "Surely fashion has nothing to do with compatibility. Let us try a different approach."

"Such as?" Damien lifted one dark eyebrow.

"Tell me how to know if a man is enamored with me. What would he say? How would he act? That sort of thing."

Damien flexed his arm, giving her hand a small squeeze. "A man who wishes to possess you would keep you close. He would compliment you and go out of his way to ensure your comfort and happiness."

Charlotte absorbed his words, then gave a nod.

"He would take every opportunity to touch you." Damien brought them to a stop and stepped in front of her. He reached out and feathered his fingers across her cheek then down her arm. "He would hunger for you."

Charlotte shivered with pleasure as a wave of warmth coursed through her. She leaned toward him. "What else might he do?" Her question came out low, husky.

"If given the chance, he would pull you into his arms." Damien gathered her against him.

Charlotte stared into his gaze, arrested by his words and actions, captured in a trance of his making. She parted her lips with a sigh. "Then what?"

Damien lowered his mouth to hers, capturing her lips beneath the soft press of his full warm ones. Completely mesmerized, Charlotte wound her arms around his neck and opened, inviting him to deepen the kiss. He suckled her lower lip, eliciting a moan from deep within her.

Damien set her apart from him, his gaze smoldering. "He will kiss you like you are the only woman alive."

Charlotte's heart hitched as Damien walked away, the heady male scent of him replaced by that of the nearby flowers. She rested her gloved fingers on her tingling lips. Why the deuce had he done that?

CHAPTER 5

Damien rode along Rotten Row beside Edgemore and his sister Lady Minerva. As was usually the case, Hyde Park bustled with people, and Rotten Row lived up to its name. Leastwise in his opinion, for so many horses and carriages traversed the route that no one actually seemed to be in motion.

Why the devil had he allowed Edgemore to drag him into this? For all the hell-raising Edgemore engaged in, he turned into a perfect gentleman when his sister was near. The fool would do anything Lady Minerva asked of him. Damien was bloody glad that he did not have a sister of his own. Or a wife for that matter. Women were too much trouble. Hell, this one was no relation of his, and still, she caused him a headache.

He cleared his throat. "Must we remain at a standstill? Could we not go around them?"

Edgemore turned to his sister. "We could choose a different path?"

She frowned back at him. "The point is to be seen, not to ride neck or nothing on some off-beaten path."

Damien squinted against the sun's rays. "The only people seeing you are those stuck directly behind us," he drawled.

Lady Minerva glanced around them. "I see your point. I suppose we could ride toward the Serpentine."

Damien wasted no time turning his mount toward the river. He'd prefer to be at the Wicked Earls' Club, but at present anywhere would be better than Rotten Row. What he wouldn't give to set his mount into a fast canter. As it was, he would have to settle for a steady gait.

He focused his attention ahead, a small smile pulling at his lips when the sparkling water came into view. It was a pleasant day, the bright sunshine illuminated the park casting shadows over the land-scape and a light breeze kept him cool.

As they neared the Serpentine, several people came into view. There were ladies strolling along the river bank with gentlemen, people relaxing upon the plush grass, and children out with their nannies, playing along the water's edge or feeding the ducks. His gaze settled on a couple sitting under a lime tree enjoying a picnic. Damien could not help but study the scene before him.

His chest tightened as the lady's features came into focus. Pale blond curls peeked out from beneath her bonnet and a rosy flush painted her cheeks as she waved her silk fan. He turned his attention to the gentleman. What the devil was Charlotte doing with Lord Jostling?

Damien's blood heated, and he turned his mount toward the pair. Jostling was no better than a parasite. He was cruel to animals and light skirts, not to mention the rumors surrounding his finances. Charlotte deserved far better. Without considering his actions, Damien jumped from his mount and grabbed Jostling by his coat, hauling him to his feet.

"What is the meaning of this?" Charlotte sprang to her feet. "Stop it at once!"

Jostling squirmed in Damien's grip. "Release me, you brute!"

Damien jerked the man by his lapels. "You are to stay away from Lady Charlotte," he said, scowling.

"That is not your decision to make." Jostling peered up at Damien. "Take your hands off me."

Damien pulled Jostling close again. "If you value your limbs, you will abandon your pursuit of her."

"People are watching." Charlotte grabbed Damien's sleeve and said, "Enough."

"He is not for you," Damien said, his gaze boring into hers.

"I will choose who I spend my time with." Charlotte tugged at Damien's hand. "Now let him go."

Damien released Jostling, then he pulled his fist back and smashed it into the parasite's jaw. As the man crumbled to the ground, Damien turned to Charlotte. "Not on my watch."

A sharp intake of breath caused both Damien and Charlotte to turn around.

"Good heavens. Why did you do that?" A wide-eyed Lady Minerva sat upon her horse with one hand resting on her chest.

"Because Lord Grayson has the manners of a farm animal," Charlotte seethed. She pivoted, returned hastily to Jostling's side, then lowered herself to the ground beside him.

Edgemore slid from his mount and went to stand

beside her. "Actually, Lord Jostling is the one lacking manners. You would serve yourself well to listen to Lord Grayson."

Charlotte slanted her glance toward Damien. "Pray tell, what is your objection to Lord Jostling?"

"He is no gentleman," Damien said.

"And you are?" Charlotte raised a pale eyebrow.

Damien's jaw tightened as he fought to suppress his rage. "You do not know the things he has done. As if whipping horses until their hides bleed is not bad enough, you should hear what he does to light—"

"That is quite enough." Edgemore nodded toward Lady Minerva who was staring at them, soaking up every word they spoke.

Damien held a hand out to Charlotte. "Allow me to return you home. I will explain everything on the way."

"I came in Lord Jostling's carriage, and that is how I shall return."

"Be reasonable." Damien stretched out his arm, moving his hand closer to her. "The man is hardly able to escort you anywhere at present."

Charlotte peered at him, her ice-blue eyes crackling. "Because of you."

"Let us not cast blame," Edgemore waved his

hand in a lazy arc. "Go with Lord Grayson and I will take care of Lord Jostling. You have my word."

Charlotte glanced back down at Jostling then returned her attention to Edgemore. "I cannot share his mount. It wouldn't be proper."

"I will walk and you can have the damn horse. Come along." Damien wiggled the fingers on his outstretched hand.

Charlotte shook her head. "No."

"Lady Charlotte can ride Minerva's horse," Edgemore said as he strolled over to his sister and helped her dismount. "We will wait for Jostling to come around then stroll around the Serpentine until you return."

"Surely you cannot object now." Lady Minerva smiled at Lady Charlotte.

"I suppose not." She stood then dusted her skirt. "Lord Edgemore, will you assist me?"

Damien released a deep breath, fisting his hands at his sides. Why did Charlotte have to be so obnoxiously difficult? Could she not see that he cared for her? He supposed not, and the fault belonged solely to him.

Edgemore gave a smile and nod as he began toward the horse.

Damien could not take his eyes from Lady Charlotte as Edgemore lifted her onto the horse. His pulse thrummed and his blood remained heated, but there was something more too—bloody hell if he wasn't jealous! He'd never stopped caring for her, despite all his efforts. Nonetheless, he could not have her. Did not want her in the way she deserved to be had.

He swung up onto his horse's saddle, taking up the reins. "Let us be on our way."

Lady Charlotte signaled her chaperones, then set the horse into a fast walk without speaking a word to Damien.

His irritation spiked. He'd be damned if the minx was going to ignore him. Not when all he'd done was protect her. Damien brought his horse beside hers. "Charlotte."

She kicked her mount, putting it into a canter.

Damien caught up in short measure. "Do be reasonable."

She shot him a seething glare. "You caused quite a scene. I imagine every tongue in London will be wagging on the morrow."

"I won't apologize."

"Of course not. I wouldn't expect anything less from you." She pushed her horse faster.

Tightening his grip on the reins, he once more

caught up to her. "Lord Jostling is a reprobate. He preys on women and has no respect for animals."

She turned up her nose. "I care not what you think of him. Save your energy and mind your own affairs."

"You became my affair when you asked for my help," Damien said, his tone low and serious. He could not allow Charlotte to make the colossal mistake of marrying Jostling. The man reminded him of his own father. How many nights had Damien cowered in a corner while his father beat his mother? He swallowed back the lump rising in his throat. Too many.

Long-ago echoes of her cries and pleas swirled through his mind. He would not allow Charlotte to have the same fate. He led his horse closer to hers and grabbed for the reins. She would hear him out whether or not she wished to. "Jostling has a reputation for abusing light skirts as well. If he enjoys whipping light skirts, what do you think he would do with a wife?"

Charlotte jerked at her horse's reins. "I do not believe you."

"Ask Edgemore. He will concur. Hell, at least half the gentlemen of the *ton* are aware of Jostling's habits," Damien said, pleading for her to hear his words, to take his warning.

"You find something wrong with all of my suitors. I do not wish to hear any more of your objections. And I bid you to keep your lies to yourself as well. Lord Jostling has been naught but a perfect gentleman. Many a lady swoons when he enters a room." Charlotte glared at him before jerking her reins. "Do return me home, then forget that I asked for your help. Forget I even exist. It should not be hard for you to do, as you've already done so once before."

Defeated—at least for the moment—Damien released the reins and let her go.

CHAPTER 6

Charlotte's gaze caught Damien's as Lord Jostling led her up the line of dancers at the Kettering Ball. She glared at him for a heartbeat before turning her attention back to her dance partner. She should never have involved herself with the unpredictable earl. Truly, her past experience with him should have been more than enough to warn her off.

Despite the passage of two full days, Charlotte could not cease thinking about Damien and the way he had acted in the park. The very nerve of him to interrupt her outing, attack Lord Jostling, and then tell such horrid stories about him. She could not help but wonder at what had possessed him to behave thusly.

In the days since, she had attended a garden party, a soirée, and a dinner party. Damien had made an appearance at all three but had not dared approach her, though neither did he ignore her. Instead, Damien spent his time staring at her and Lord Jostling as if they were the most interesting and offensive things he had ever seen.

Lord Jostling twirled her before separating from her. As she returned to her place in the line, she cast a glance to where Damien had been standing sentinel near a large floor to ceiling window. He peered back at her but did not budge from his post.

Every time she hazarded a glance, she found Damien nearby with his attention honed in on her and Lord Jostling. It made her nerves crackle and caused her blood to heat. Worse, despite her vexation with him a deep down part of her thrilled at his attention. She must be the most awful sort of lady to find any pleasure in his attention. More so, considering her desire to wed another.

Charlotte could not say that she loved Lord Jostling; however, he was the most attentive of her suitors and she enjoyed his company. The man had done nothing to give her pause—not even after Damien had attacked him.

In fact, Lord Jostling had called on her, offering

apologies and the gift of a rare orchid. The very thing Damien should have done, less the gift, of course. And yet, she found herself still drawn to him like a moth to the very flame that would cause its demise.

The music ended and Charlotte returned her attention to Lord Jostling as the next dance in their set began.

Lord Jostling pulled her into his arms as the first chords of a waltz filled the ballroom. "Ignore him."

"It's difficult when he won't cease staring at us." Charlotte cautioned a glance in Damien's direction, and he scowled. Even from such a distance, she could read the displeasure in his eyes. They fairly crackled as she notched her chin defiantly.

"Look at me," Lord Jostling said.

Charlotte brought her gaze back to his.

"He will soon grow tired of playing nursemaid. In the meantime, I have set up a little distraction." Lord Jostling grinned. "There she is now."

Charlotte drew her brows together. A lithe woman with golden tresses piled on top of her head took hold of Damien's arm. Charlotte had the sudden urge to march across the ballroom and insert herself between them as Damien bestowed a roguish grin on the woman. Before she could act so foolish, Lord Jostling guided her from the dance floor.

"Lady Constantine will keep him distracted while we sneak away for a bit."

Charlotte could not help but glance back over her shoulder. The harlot had her paws all over Damien in the most inappropriate way. Were they familiar with one another? Perhaps the woman hoped to find herself beneath his bedclothes? Anger and something more akin to jealousy spread through Charlotte. What the devil was the matter with her? It was as though she'd lost all sense.

Tearing her gaze from the pair, she turned back to Lord Jostling, her grip on his arm a little tighter than it had been.

"I have a surprise for you," Lord Jostling said.

Charlotte gave him a smile. "You needn't go to any trouble on my behalf."

"You are worth all the trouble in the world, Lady Charlotte. I intend to spoil you every chance I have." He patted her gloved hand where it rested on his coat sleeve as he swept her into the hallway.

Excitement bubbled up within her and shoved all remaining thoughts of Damien into the shadows of her mind. He was her past; Lord Jostling would be her future. A future she found herself desperate to begin. She turned a dazzling smile on him. "You flatter me, my lord. I cannot wait to see what you have done."

"You deserve flattery." Lord Jostling chuckled. He led Charlotte into the orangerie then down the winding path to the back of the room. He did not speak as they strolled; only rested his hand over hers on his crooked arm.

The smell of citrus engulfed her and the warmth of the orangerie wrapped around her, calming what remained of her irritation with Damien. As it were his words from the park haunted her—echoed through her mind from time to time. She'd studied Lord Jostling, watched his interactions with others and read far too much into the way he treated her, touched her, spoke to her—Damien had to have been lying for Lord Jostling dispelled no indications of cruelty. She resolved to enjoy her time with Lord Jostling. No more would she allow Damien, or his words, to interfere.

Her breath caught when Lord Jostling brought her to a stop. There before her was a small table sequestered within a group of fruit trees. A candelabra and two champagne flutes sat upon the crisp red tablecloth. Perhaps he would propose to her this evening? A prospect that should cause her joy, however, at the moment she experienced none.

Forcing a brilliant smile, she turned to Lord Jostling. "How perfect."

"It pales in comparison to you." Lord Jostling lifted a flute and handed it to her.

Charlotte's cheeks warmed as she accepted the glass. She doubted she would ever grow accustomed to receiving such compliments. Far too many years had passed since she was a flirtatious debutant.

Lord Jostling retrieved the second flute and held it out. "A toast to us."

"To us." Charlotte grinned before taking a drink of the sweet bubbly liquor.

"Dance with me." Lord Jostling pulled her scandalously close with his free arm.

Charlotte stiffened at their close proximity. She wanted to enjoy this—to soak him up—but she could not relax. Forcing herself to follow his lead, she took another swallow of champagne as they swayed together.

Lord Jostling stopped moving but did not release her. "Finish your drink." He grinned before draining his own flute of the golden liquid.

She did as he bid, then allowed him to take her flute and place it on the table.

"Better?" He asked, as he rubbed the back of his fingers across her cheek.

When had he removed his gloves? Charlotte nodded. "Yes." Though in truth she was far from better. For reasons she could not explain, her nerves were on end. Her chest tight and stomach heavy. She would welcome the heady effects of the champagne if they ever caught up to her.

"I am going to kiss you now." Lord Jostling brought his lips to hers.

His mouth brushed hers and Charlotte closed her eyes, waiting for the headiness she knew a kiss brought. Lord Jostling's lips moved over hers, suckling, tantalizing, daring her to deepen the kiss. Still, Charlotte felt nothing—certainly not the desire to kiss him more fully.

This, too, was Damien's fault. He had her so upset that she could not allow herself to focus on Lord Jostling. The dratted rogue! Even now, she could smell his unique scent of sandalwood and bergamot tangled with raw masculinity.

The hairs on the back of her neck prickled, and she opened her eyes. She pulled her lips from Lord Jostling's and inhaled sharply. Damien strode toward them, a fierce scowl twisting his features.

Charlotte stepped out of Lord Jostling's

embrace and marched toward Damien. She'd not allow him to harm Lord Jostling again. No more would the devil interfere in her affairs. She'd had enough of longing for him, of desiring him, more than her share of heartache at his hands. She placed her hands on her hips and peered at him. "This is a private moment. No one invited you."

"You are an unwed lady." Having reached her, Damien took her elbow. "You do not get to have private moments."

She jerked her arm, but he did not release his hold on her. "You have no say in the matter."

"We shall see about that." Damien gave another tug, setting her in motion.

"The devil we will." She dug in her heels, fighting to remain in place.

"Don't waste your energy fighting the ox," Lord Jostling said. "I will call on you tomorrow."

Charlotte felt like she should stomp on Damien's foot. Demand to be released. Pull her arm free. Anything other than accepting his brutish behavior. Instead, she simply allowed him to take her from the orangerie.

Knowing Damien as she did, nothing she could do would sway him from his course. Best to stop resisting and allow him to return her to the safety of her parents.

She'd expected Damien to take her straight back to the ballroom. When he instead led her through a side door and out into the garden, her anger bloomed afresh. The nerve of him denying her stolen moment with Lord Jostling and then forcing her into one with him. She jerked free, spinning around on him. "You can rest at ease. I am returning to my parents."

Damien's gaze softened, pleading silently with her. "He is the worst sort of man. Nothing good can come of your courtship."

Charlotte turned away, her heart hammering. "No, you are."

"Charlotte, listen to me." Damien approached her, his gaze never leaving hers. "Please."

"No, you listen to me. Lord Jostling has been the perfect gentleman." Charlotte pointed her finger at him. "I like him, and there is nothing you can do to stop me from seeing him." Charlotte held her ground as Damien drew closer. "We have a comfortable companionship, and I believe he would make a fine husband."

"Is that truly what you want? A comfortable

companionship?" Damien swept his gaze down the length of her body.

Charlotte ignored the heat rising within her and glared at him. "What more could I ask for? Love?" Cynicism laced her voice. "I believe I have already tried that," she said.

"You could at least strive for passion," Damien said, then captured her lips in a crushing kiss.

Charlotte's belly fluttered and her knees went weak as she opened for him. Her tongue slid against his, the heat of her anger giving way to a fierce longing. She wanted him—all of him—and yet she could not have him. She pulled away and pivoted for the house.

"Tell me, do his kisses disarm you? Do they make your thighs quiver? Does your breath come in pants?" Damien asked.

Charlotte did not look back, she could not, for if she did, Damien would see the answers without her speaking a word.

CHAPTER 7

Damien tried to enjoy the buxom wench seated on his lap as he drained his fourth—or was it his fifth?—tumbler of scotch. After Charlotte had fled from him, he'd gone to the Wicked Earls' Club, determined to drink her away.

The wench squirmed, her bottom teasing his cock. The action should have caused him to take her upstairs. Bloody hell, Charlotte had gotten to him—ruined him. He'd not run about like a green lad in love.

Love?

No, he couldn't be in love. He cared for her, just like he had in the past, and wanted to protect her, but nothing more.

"Allow me to distract you, my lord," The wench

whispered near his ear, her breath tickling his hair as she ran her hand up his thigh. An action that on another night would have aroused him.

Damien sighed, reaching for his tumbler, and said, "Not tonight, love."

She pouted, then stood. "As you wish."

Damien turned to Edgemore. "What say you we go visit some other haunts and see what we might get into?"

Edgemore downed his scotch, then stood. "After you."

"I'll come along as well." Westcliff set his tumbler down and rose to his feet.

Damien had not caroused with the other earls of the club—Edgemore excluded—as they all tended to avoid each other outside of their sanctuary. It was one of the rules, but what did he care? He'd never been one to follow rules anyway. He nodded at Westcliff before heading toward the door. "The more the merrier, so long as you can keep up with us."

Westcliff chuckled good-naturedly. "Fear not, Grayson, I'm no slug."

Damien, Edgemore, and Westcliff stepped out onto the street. Despite the late hour, carriages, horses, and light skirts filled the walkways and streets. Damien retrieved his flask from his inside coat pocket and took a copious drink.

"Should we hail a hackney?" Edgemore asked.

"No," Damien answered, handing his flask to Edgemore.

"Then what do you have in mind?" Westcliff stepped around a putrid puddle.

Damien sniggered. "I have yet to decide."

"There is always White's, or if you want something seedier we could pay a visit to The Two Sevens," Edgemore suggested, before passing the flask to Westcliff.

Westcliff held up his hand. "I've got my own." He pulled the shiny metal flask from his coat.

"Something other than gambling and betting books is in order," Damien said. His normal activities would do nothing to keep Charlotte from his mind, and bloody hell he did not want to think about her.

Westcliff grinned. "Very well, how about we pay a call at Madam Doeshy's fine establishment?"

"So we might all wake with fire in our groins? I think not." Edgemore laughed. "Though, if women are what you have in mind, we could go to a private party I happen to be aware of. The type of party where women are clean, half-clothed, and willing to satisfy your every inclination."

"I could use a warm and willing wench." Westcliff looked to Damien. "But then, I could have had that inside of the club."

"You are welcome to go back in." Damien shook his head. "I am not in the mood for female entertainment."

"If not gaming and women, then what?" Edgemore swayed, nearly bumping against a wall before righting himself and taking another deep swig of liquor.

Damien grinned. "Let us retrieve mounts and go raise hell. We will just see where the night takes us."

"Perhaps we should race?" Westcliff gave a challenging nod.

Damien quickened his pace. "Perfect." A bit of wild and reckless sport should prove a wonderful distraction.

Only it did not. After riding neck or nothing across the English countryside thoughts of Charlotte still dominated his mind. So, much as he wished to ignore her, he simply couldn't. Not when she was tossing herself headfirst into a life of abuse and misery. He retrieved his flask and took a deep swallow. "I have something to take care of."

"We will accompany you," Edgemore said, glancing at Damien from where he sat upon his stallion. "But do tell us what the mission involves?"

"Jostling," Damien said. "I am going to pay him a call."

Westcliff arched a brow. "Whatever for?" he asked.

"To deliver a warning," Damien said, taking another long draw from his flask.

Edgemore whistled, long and low. "You do care for the chit."

"What chit?" Westcliff asked, glancing back and forth at them from where he rode between them.

Damien put his flask back in his pocket. "No woman deserves the hell he brings."

"You diverted from telling us that you care. This is serious. I dare say it may be love." Edgemore took a swig of his own whiskey.

"Rubbish." Damien shook his head though he was beginning to suspect the same thing. He'd never admit to being in love, not to himself, and certainly not to them. "Do let us find Jostling and quit this nonsensical conversation."

Edgemore chuckled as he tucked his liquor into his coat. "Where do you suggest we look? Last I knew the reportage had been banned from all of London's finer establishments."

"Touché, I saw him at White's this morning," Westcliff said.

"I was referring to brothels," Edgemore drawled.

Westcliff flicked his reins. "Yes, of course, though I've heard tell that he frequently visits a brothel in St. Giles."

"Do you have a name?" Damien asked.

"Not that I can recall, though I do remember something about Seven Dials." Westcliff attempted to take a swig from his flask, then tossed it to the ground. "Bloody hell, it's empty."

"Stop whining, we'll stop by a gin house." Damien tapped his heels against his horse, setting it into a fast canter. He did not know what he would do or say to Jostling, but he certainly had to do something. There was no way he could sit back and allow the parasite to wed Charlotte. He'd kill the spineless weasel first.

After reaching Seven Dials, Damien, along with Edgemore and Westcliff, entered the first brothel they found asking after and looking for Jostling. They came away empty, not a soul within claimed to have ever seen Jostling. The same was true of the second and third.

Discouraged, Damien strolled back out into the stinking street, doing his best to avoid stepping in anything untoward. He glanced at Westcliff. "Are you quite certain you heard right?"

Westcliff gave a hard nod then reached out his hand. "Give me your flask."

Damien shook his head.

"I won't drain it."

Damien reached into his coat and produced the shiny metal flask. "You can bloody well keep the damn thing if you just remember the name of the brothel."

"I know of one that caters to all sorts of tastes, not far from here. Seems the type of place a man like Jostling would frequent." Edgemore swung back onto his saddle. "Come along."

Damien mounted without a word and directed his horse to follow Edgemore. A short distance later, down a couple of Filthy streets, past prostitutes and street urchins, Edgemore drew his mount to a stop in front of a dilapidated two-story building. The roof sagged, several shutters were missing while other's hung loose, and the old wooden door wore a coating of moss.

A shudder went through him as he turned to

Edgemore. "This place is not fit for rats. How do you know of it?"

Edgemore jumped down from his horse. "Never mind all that."

"I must admit to being rather curious myself," Westcliff said as he dismounted.

Rising voices from within drifted out to the street as Damien and Westcliff awaited Edgemore's explanation.

"Is lordship done it. Bloodied me mouth, he did!" A shrill female voice filled the darkened street.

Damien would wager they had found Jostling. He turned and stormed toward the entrance. Grabbing the ramshackle door, he threw it open and stepped inside. His gaze ceased on Jostling who presently tossed a pouch he could only assume held coin toward an older woman.

"'Tis more than enough for her trouble," Jostling said.

"Ain't no coin worth spending me time with ye," a woman shouted from somewhere off to his left.

Damien turned his attention in the direction of her voice. His breath caught. Good God, the girl could not be a day over eighteen—if she were even that. Her lip was split and swollen, blood smeared across her face and exposed chest. "What the devil happened?" Damien shouted.

"Said I did no suck 'im good as I should. Said me teeth were in the way. Then he tried ta knock um out. The bas—"

Damien lunged toward Jostling and shoved him into a table. Jostling stumbled, losing his balance and falling to the plank board floor. The whores and patrons crowding the room spread out, clearing the space as Damien hoisted Jostling back to his feet and slammed him against a wall.

Jostling stared at Damien, anger shining in his soulless eyes. "This is none of your concern."

"Make no mistake, my actions have little to do with what atrocities you committed here," Damien ground out the words. "Though you deserve far worse than a thrashing for what you've done. I will see to it personally that you meet your end if you go near Lady Charlotte again."

Jostling's eyes rounded. "I am going to marry her."

"The devil you are!" Damien pulled Jostling toward him then slammed him back into the wall. He leaned in close and said in a deadly tone, "I will kill you with my bare hands." Damien released the reprobate, turned and strolled back toward his friends. "This place reeks, let us be gone."

Once they stepped back onto the street, Edgemore said, "Might we find that gin house now?"

"Perhaps we should return to The Wicked earls' Club," Westcliff suggested.

Damien mounted his horse, then glanced at the others. "I don't bloody well care what you do. As for me, I intend to drink copious amounts of liquor and raise hell all night long."

"Will you be joining us, Westcliff?"

"I'd never pass up such an opportunity."

Edgemore chuckled as he swung onto his horse. "Then let us be on our way."

CHAPTER 8

*D*amien attempted to open his eyes despite the throbbing in his head. He managed small slits, squinting against the bright rays of sun flooding his bedchamber. Bloody hell his head was throbbing, and what the devil was making so much noise? When he tried to sit up the room spun around him causing him to lie back down.

After gaining some of his bearings, Damien pushed himself up in the bed and forced his eyes to focus. Edgemore lay haphazardly across his chaise, snoring like the devil. When the pounding from above started a fresh, Damien slid from his bed. He was going to pummel whoever was responsible for the racket.

Still dressed in his white shirt and breeches from

last night, he followed the thudding and banging sounds that now vibrated through him. Bloody hell, he must have drunk half the swill in London last night. He could not recall a time he'd ever been so hungover.

Holding his head to try and drown out some of the offending noise, he made his way down the hallway. By the sound of it, whatever was causing the ruckus was in the attic. He tossed open the door and started up the stairs, one careful step at a time.

Damien paused at the top of the stairs and peered across the attic. His gaze arrested on the offending noise maker. What the hell was going on? He could not be seeing what he thought he did. It was impossible, at the very least highly improbable. He blinked once, twice, three times before he refocused his gaze. Still, it remained.

He pivoted a touch too hastily and his head began to spin again. He was going to beat Edgemore for this. After regaining his balance, Damien returned to his bedchamber. He marched up to the chaise Edgemore slept upon and kicked at his foot. "Edgemore, get up!"

Edgemore stirred but did not rise.

"Open your damn eyes," Damien yelled, kicking at his friend's foot once more.

"What the devil is wrong with you?" Edgemore peered up at Damien, without making any effort to sit upright. He lay a hand across his forehead, allowing his eyes to drift closed. "Can't you make that bloody racket stop?"

Damien cleared his throat. "That bloody noise happens to be your fault."

"The devil it is." Edgemore opened his eyes.

"Come along, I will show you." Damien marched to the door before turning back to find Edgemore still reclining on the chaise. "Get your sorry ass up and follow me."

"Can we not do this later? Send a servant to deal with the racket. A tonic would be most welcome as well." Edgemore dropped his arm over his eyes. "My head feels as though it will split in half."

"Edgemore," Damien drew out the end syllable, his voice low and menacing. If he did not have such a terrible hangover himself, he would drag the man unto the attic. As it were, Damien could barely make his own body move.

Edgemore pushed to his feet. "Since you insist."

Damien stepped out into the hallway and led Edgemore up to the attic. He stopped at the top of the stairs, his gaze moving from the irate animal to Edgemore. "Care to explain?"

The horse reared up, nostrils flaring then brought its hooves down hard enough to vibrate the floor beneath Damien's feet.

He scowled at Edgemore as his head began pounding afresh.

"I am quite certain this is not of my doing." Edgemore turned, starting back down the stairs.

Damien caught him by the shirt collar. "Be that as it may, the horse belongs to you."

"What happened to Westcliff?" Edgemore turned then glanced around the attic. "Perhaps he dared me or decided to play a trick on us?"

"I cannot claim to remember," Damien said. "And nor does it make any difference."

"Calm down old fellow." Edgemore attempted to sooth the horse as he took a few steps toward the animal. "Perhaps Westcliff could tell us how Crusader got up here. I'd bloody well like to know."

Damien huffed a breath. It would be a wonder if any of them could recall the events of last night. Raising hell and suffering for it come morning was nothing new for them; however, Damien could not remember the last time he forgot the majority of an evening. The last thing he could recall was racing, neck or nothing, about London's outskirts with Westcliff and Edgemore.

The memory of slamming Jostling against a wall seeped into his mind. It was quite fuzzy, but there all the same. Then they had returned to London, gone after more liquor. "You dared him to deface a statue."

Edgemore chuckled. "Ah, I do recall it now. He painted a mustache on the marble horse. Then we went toward the outskirts of town."

"I do not recall a thing thereafter," Damien said.

Why the devil had he allowed himself to get so foxed? His argument with Lady Charlotte bore the blame for his actions. Indeed, she had driven him to self-destruction exactly as she had when they were younger.

Well, not quite the same. Back then, he had chosen to embrace the wilder side of life rather than offering for her hand in marriage. Now, he wished to save her from herself, but she'd not allow him to. How ironic.

Damien could take some comfort in the knowledge he'd gone after Jostling, gave the man a warning he ought not to ignore. Somehow he doubted the parasite would heed him, but what more could he do when Charlotte refused to listen to his warnings? He could not ponder the issue at present. His head pounded far too much for productive deducing and there was the matter of Crusader in his attic.

Damien turned what little focus he currently possessed toward Edgemore. "He's your mount, surely you are not afraid of him. Grab the damned bridle and let us be done with this nonsense."

Edgemore inched toward the horse, cooing gentle words to the beast. Slowly he reached out attempting to grab the bridle. Crusader reared and snorted. "He's duced angry."

"As am I." Damien scowled, moving closer to the horse.

"I've got him," Edgemore victoriously called out before Damien could reach them.

Damien stared toward the far corner, where Edgemore held Crusader by the bridle. "Wonderful. Now, see him to the stables so that I might regain a modicum of peace."

"Who wants peace when life is exceedingly more fun without it?" Edgemore led the horse toward the stairs. "I aspire never to have peace."

Damien rolled the sentiment around his throbbing brain. He'd spent all of his adult life avoiding settling down—embracing chaos and recklessness. Each day brought more: gambling, booze, women, fighting, reckless pranks, and adventuring... Perhaps he'd grown weary of living such a wild existence. Maybe the time had come to settle down.

When they approached the attic stairs, Crusader snorted and bucked his back hooves causing Damien to still.

"There, there," Edgemore soothed.

Damien stepped aside so that Edgemore could lead Crusader down the stairs, then followed once he had a large enough berth to ensure he would not get kicked. As he absorbed the scene unfolding before him, he imagined what an alternate life would be like.

Had he offered for Charlotte all those years ago, he would not be presently removing a horse from his attic. He'd likely have an heir and a spare. Perhaps a beautiful daughter as well. One with the same silvery hair and striking blue eyes as her mother.

Each night, instead of raising hell, he would snuggle into bed with the same woman—with Charlotte. A slow smile spread across his lips at the notion of it all. A fortnight ago the very thought would have repulsed him. But in light of recent events, domesticity did not seem so bad. Hell with Charlotte the idea actually held some appeal.

"Almost there." Edgemore's voice cut through Damien's thoughts.

"Fredrickson, open the door." Damien strolled around Edgemore and Crusader as they neared the main stairwell. He found the butler, meeting the man's rounded eyes. He could only begin to imagine what title would go on below stairs this afternoon. Not that he gave a damn what his servants thought.

The aging butler turned, pulled the door open, then gazed back at them with disbelief in his eyes. Over the years Fredrickson had seen many odd things because of Damien's shenanigans, but never anything remotely as odd as this. Damien gave the man credit for maintaining his composure as they marched past. He wasn't certain he'd be able to manage the same if roles were reversed.

Edgemore led Crusader onto the porch. A footman rushed over. "Allow me," the livery-clad man said, taking the bridle as though there were nothing at all unusual about the events unfolding before him.

"Please see the horse stabled and fed." Damien grinned, suddenly finding humor in the absurdity of it all.

"Immediately, sir." The footman gave a bow then led the horse away.

Suddenly everything seemed so clear. He did want to settle down and he knew how best to protect

Charlotte from Jostling as well as ensure both of their futures were happy.

He shook his head, his heart beating a bit faster. Why ever would anyone choose to live in such a way as he had? He must have been daft to embrace such foolishness. More so for failing to deduce the answer to his problem with Charlotte. To the devil with his fears, his club, and anything else that might stand in his way.

Damien clapped Edgemore on the shoulder. "You are welcome to take a guest room until you are ready to travel home. I have something I must attend to."

If Charlotte would not heed his warnings about Jostling, then he would have to take drastic measures to save her from certain misery—perhaps to save them both.

Charlotte strode into the parlor, not at all sure why Damien had come to call. She'd wager he wished to harass her further over Lord Jostling. Well, if that was his intention, he would be sorely disappointed. Her mind had been decided and nothing he could say or do would change a thing.

The objections he'd assigned for each of her suitors had initially amused her, but the way he attacked Lord Jostling went too far. The very idea that such a sweet man could act with such cruelty was absurd. She'd not allow Damien to continue with his absurd lies. She steeled herself for the coming confrontation as she strolled across the room.

She took the chair opposite him and met his gaze. "Lord Grayson." She nodded politely despite the ire ravaging her insides.

"Lord Grayson?" he asked, arching a brow, his tone uncertain. "I do not believe you have ever addressed me thusly when in private. I must confess, I do not like it."

"We are not in private," she said, indicating Lady Oxford, who'd trailed in behind her and stationed herself in the far corner near the fireplace.

"Regardless, I prefer you call me Damien. We are old friends, if nothing else."

Charlotte pressed her lips together, gave a slight shake of her head. "I no longer wish to be informal with you. I am to be Lord Jostling's wife. The marriage contracts will be signed this afternoon."

Damien sprang from his chair. "You must not—," he began, but she cut him off.

"Quiet." Charlotte held up a hand. "As I was saying, the contracts will be signed this afternoon and our engagement formally announced at tonight's dinner party." She could not begin to understand why he objected so fiercely, but it had to stop here—this very moment.

"He is certain to make you miserable, Charlotte."

Damien stood, ran a hand through his dark hair, sat back down. "Charlotte, you must believe me."

Why did he cling so fiercely to his objections? He had no wish to marry her himself, never had. Did he find some perverse joy in torturing her? A sick satisfaction in knowing that her heart still ached for him that he did not wish to risk losing to another man?

God, she still loved him. She prayed, in time, to love Lord Jostling even half as much. Prayed harder that time would heal the wounds Damien had left on her soul. She had to remain firm and set boundaries with him. "Do refrain from addressing me so. From now on, it must be Lady Charlotte."

Damien strolled over to her, his gaze finding hers. "You cannot mean that," he said.

She stood, glaring at him. "Why do you insist on painting him as a monster?"

"Because, dammit, he is."

Warning flashed in Damien's cocoa eyes, but Charlotte saw something else there too. A warmth she dare not be fooled by. She glared angrily then pivoted on her heel to storm from the room.

Damien reached out taking her hand, stopping her. "Charlotte, I care deeply for you. I want you to be happy and safe."

She opened her mouth to argue, but paused as

pain and something else, something more tender, filled his gaze. *Love?* Her heart hitched, a lump rising in her throat. "I...I can't." She made a weak attempt to get free.

"Can't what? Believe that I have your best interest in mind? That I truly wish for you to be happy? That I do care deeply for you?" He stepped closer, bringing his body against hers. "I have always cared."

She blew out a deep breath, her insides trembling. "Then why did you break my heart?" He voice quivered and she hated herself for it. She'd never intended to drudge up the past. It served no purpose now—they could not go back. Not now that she had accepted Lord Jostling's offer.

Damien rubbed small circles on the backs of her gloved hands. "I was protecting you."

"From what?" She asked, drawing her brows together in befuddlement.

He averted his gaze and then said in a voice so low she could scarcely believe what she'd heard. "From me."

Her heart nearly arrested at the raw honesty he displayed. "I did not need protecting from you." She reached out, placing her hand on his cheek and guiding his gaze back to hers. "You were all I thought about, all I wanted."

He stared at her, his emotions shielded once more. "You were a wide-eyed debutante with your mind set on marriage, and I a rogue determined never to marry." He released her hand and stepped away. "I would have ruined you. And I cared too much for you to let that happen."

She nibbled her lower lip as his words sank in. How many nights...years...had she wondered at his reason for turning away from her. She'd always believed that he had been toying with her, amusing himself with the gullible debutante. Never had she imagined—let alone believed that he might have cared for her. Still... "You are an earl. Did it not occur to you that you must marry at some point?"

"Why? So I might produce an heir? I care not what happens to the title." Damien moved close to the window, his attention trained on the view it provided. "My father was a miserable bastard. I have no idea how to be a husband and father, and no wish to follow his example."

Charlotte drew close, resting her hand on his shoulder. "You are not your father."

Damien stiffened. "You have no idea. I am a wicked man given to gambling, women, and horses. I enjoy my liquor and raise hell every chance I get. All traits I share with my father. Who's to say that I would not continue following his example within the confines of marriage?"

He paused as though waiting for Charlotte to speak. She gave a weak smile not at all sure how to respond.

"Did you know that he beat my mother on a regular basis? Damien asked. "He slapped her around and yelled at her every chance he got?"

Her heart melted at the hurt in his voice, the pain in his eyes. She wanted to wrap him in her embrace and love away all of the doubt and hurt he'd suffered. Why hadn't he been honest with her before now? She would have loved him despite it all. Would have embraced a life with him.

"Perhaps you are a bit wicked, but you have a soul." She stepped around him so that she could gaze into his tender eyes. "Damien, you are not your father. You said yourself that you care for me. I'd wager he never gave a fig for anyone."

Damien tipped his head back and closed his eyes for a heartbeat. "I did care for you...I still do." He locked gazes with her. "If you believe nothing else, believe that."

Charlotte could not hide the ghost of a smile

curving her lips. "I cared for you as well. In fact, I loved you. I still do." The words tumbled from her mouth before she could stop them. Maybe she hadn't wanted to leave them unspoken.

"Do not tie yourself to Jostling." Damien pulled her into his arms. "Marry me."

How many nights had she laid awake longing to hear him speak those words? He had been her every dream back then. Even now, even after the pain and anguish he'd caused her, she loved him. She'd be a fool to try denying it, but dare she believe him?

It mattered not, he could not matter. Lord Jostling was her future. Damien her past. The agreement was already drawn up; it was too late to change things now. She fought the tears welling in her eyes as she stared back at Damien. "Do not make this harder than it already is. I get on well with Lord Jostling and have already agreed to become his wife."

"Nothing has been signed. No official announcements made." He nuzzled his head where her earlobe met her neck and dropped a kiss on the delicate skin. "Choose me. I swear I will spend the rest of our lives doing all I can to be a good husband, to keep you safe, and make you happy."

God, how he tempted her. Another gentle caress

and she would be reduced to dough in his hands. The man infuriated her, but he also stirred her passions as no other ever had. Charlotte drew in a breath and stepped from his embrace. "Our chance has long passed. Please take your leave." She turned her back to him, fighting for composure.

"Charlotte, I want to be your husband. Never again do I want to wake to find a friend snoring across my room or a horse in my attic—"

"A horse?"

"Indeed, and before you ask me to explain, I haven't a clue how it got there." He took her hands in his and gave a gentle squeeze. "The point is, I want to settle down. You made me see that there is more to life."

"Do you love me?" Charlotte searched his gaze, finding her answer in the warmth of his eyes before he spoke a single word.

"Love is not an emotion I am familiar with." He swallowed hard. "I think about you all the time. There is not enough liquor in England to keep you off my mind. I worry about you and wish to protect you. I desire you and want you with me."

Charlotte nodded as tears collected in her eyes. "Please, do go on."

"I want you to be my first, my last, and everything

in-between for the rest of my days, Charlotte. I believe that is love."

She rose onto her toes and pressed her lips to his. When she pulled back, her heart nearly burst with joy at the love reflecting back at her. How could she marry Lord Jostling when Damien owned her heart and soul? How could she wed another after Damien professed his love for her? She couldn't— repercussions be damned.

"Marry me?" Damien dropped a kiss on her forehead.

"Under one condition." She twirled her fingers in the hair at the back of his neck.

His gaze smoldered. "I will do anything you desire. Give you all that you need."

She brought her mouth close to his ear. "I do not want a good husband."

His muscled jaw tightened. "You don't?"

She dropped a kiss on his neck, then smiled at him mischievously. "I want a wicked husband. One who ignites my passions."

"I assure you that I am fit for the challenge." He captured her lips in a wicked, soul-consuming kiss and she melted against him, taking all that he offered.

EPILOGUE

London, three months later

Damien rolled away from Charlotte, collapsing against the pillows, his breath coming in pants and body slick with sweat. Completely sated, for the moment, he pulled his countess into his arms.

Charlotte nestled her head against his bare chest and he trailed his fingers up and down her arm in a gentle caress. She released a soft breath, her languid body molding against his. There was nowhere in the world Damien would rather be.

Charlotte drew little circles on his chest. "Do you ever regret giving up your freedom for me?"

He rolled to face her, and swept his gaze slowly

over her naked body. Desire reignited, making him ache for her once more. It had been that way from the beginning and would always be so. "Never."

She smiled up at him, her expression mulish. "Not even when your friends come to call and share their exploits?"

"None of their adventures compare to what I share with you, love. Have no doubt that you are where I want to be." He dropped a tender kiss on the crown of her head. Since their wedding, he and Charlotte had not spent a single night apart. He craved her like no other vice he'd ever had. But not just at night, not simply for physical enjoyment either.

During their waking hours, he took every opportunity to be in her company. She challenged him, excited him, ignited his passion, and so much more. He still had a hard time believing that he'd almost been fool enough to let her go.

"Sometimes I wonder if I am dreaming. I fear that I will awaken and you will simply vanish from my life." She played with the downy thatch of hair on his chest. "I know it is silly, yet I cannot help myself."

"It's not silly, love. I experience the same fear." She glanced up at him, the emotion in her eyes nearly overwhelming him. What the devil had he done to deserve a woman like her? Sweet and compassionate with a wicked streak he'd never tire of. He was a lucky man indeed, and entirely undeserving.

She rose up on her elbows, eyeing him with possessive, shameless desire. "Allow me to ease your fears by showing you just how much I love you, my lord."

His blood ignited as she slid her naked body against his. "As you wish, My Lady."

She placed her legs on either side of his hips, then sank down on his hard length.

Damien released a deep, possessive moan as she began rocking back and forth in perfect rhythm with his racing heart. Unable to stop himself he reached for her, wrapping his hand behind her head to tangle his fingers in her long blond tresses. He guided her down to him and captured her lips with his.

Staring into her eyes, he said, "I love you."

"I love you too."

Her words came out husky, the sound adding to his pleasure. His body tightened as hers began to pulse and throb around his cock. She released a throaty moan, her hips moving faster and his resistance fractured.

Completely satisfied, he pulled her down against his chest and wrapped his arms tightly around her. "You have thoroughly convinced me. Next time, I will endeavor to do the same for you."

She laughed, the delicate sound warming his soul. "I shall never grow tired of being wicked with you."

Damien stroked her soft hair back from her cheeks. "I shall never grow weary of being with you in any way. You are my heart, my soul, the very breath I breathe. Never doubt it for a single moment." He laid a kiss on her head, inhaling her sweet scent.

Then Damien Archer, the Earl of Grayson held his wife a little tighter, looking forward to a life of adventure and fiery passion with the woman who fulfilled his soul—the Wicked Earls' Club be damned, for the rest of his days, and nights, Charlotte would be his sanctuary.

Keep reading for an excerpt from Amanda's next
book in the Wicked Earls' Club!

In the frosted heart of a Regency Christmas, the Earl
of Edgemore, Blake Fox, embodies the very essence
of a roguish aristocrat. With his devil-may-care atti-
tude and a charm that disarms, Blake is accustomed
to a life where his whims dictate his actions, apologies be damned. However, this Christmas, the winds
of fate blow a fiery Scottish lass, Carstine Greer, into
the picturesque world of the Edgemore estate,
setting the stage for an encounter as unpredictable
as a winter storm. Mistaken for a mere maid, Cars-

tine's fiery spirit clashes with Blake's unchecked arrogance, igniting a vow of revenge that could melt even the coldest of hearts.

Unbeknownst to both, the gears of fate are further turned by the meddling hands of Lady Minerva, Blake's sister, whose matchmaking endeavors are as relentless as they are well-intentioned. As the Yuletide season unfolds, the estate becomes a stage for mischievous plots, mistaken identities, and unexpected alliances. Amidst the chaos, the lines between revenge and attraction, begin to blur, challenging everything Blake and Carstine thought they knew about love and each other.

Beneath the mistletoe and magic of Christmas, will the wicked Earl find himself ensnared in his own game, or will the fiery Scottish lass's quest for vengeance lead her to a different prize altogether? Can the magic of Christmas and the meddlesome strategies of Lady Minerva weave a love story that not even a roguish earl can escape?

Amidst festive revelries and heartfelt confessions, Blake and Carstine's icy encounters may just melt into a love that defies expectations.

CHAPTER 1

England, 1816

"ollocks," Carstine Greer cussed as her ankle twisted beneath her. She dropped to the frozen ground at the side of the road and inhaled sharply at the ensuing pain. Reaching for her hem, she began pulling up her skirt to inspect her injury.

"Ach," she seethed as she worked to free her foot from the confines of her boot. Each movement sent unpleasant jolts of white-hot pain through her ankle and up her leg. She glared at the offending icy patch that had caused her misery.

Tossing her boot aside, Carstine feathered her fingers over the angry, red, and swollen skin of her ankle. Despite the pain she knew would follow, Carstine forced herself to wiggle her toes then flex her foot.

Good, the bone hadn't fractured, though she was still in a great deal of pain. She'd earned herself a nasty sprain, to be sure.

She'd wager this would not have happened if her parents had allowed her to remain in Scotland.

Why the devil had Mother been so insistent that Carstine come to England? She did not care about English society, nor was she in any hurry to wed. She wasn't opposed to husband-hunting, but saw no reason why she couldn't do it in the highlands. A braw Scottish man would suit her best, she thought, as she put her boot back on with care.

The pounding of horse hooves pulled her from her misery. She glanced down the snow-blanketed road. A rider was racing toward her at breakneck speed. She caught a glimpse of the gentleman as he flew past, the tails of his greatcoat flapping in the wind, before bringing his mount to a halt then turning back toward her.

Carstine stared unabashedly as the rider made his way back to her. He was tall and muscular beneath his greatcoat with broad shoulders, a strong jaw, and curious blue eyes framed in thick lashes.

The man sat expertly upon a great chestnut beast of a horse. A fine specimen indeed—both the horse and its rider.

Carstine gave a slight grin then nodded as the stranger met her gaze.

The man nodded in return before moving his attention to her ankle. His eyebrows scrunched as he inspected her. "You're injured."

"Aye." She nodded then cringed as she finished pulling her boot back on. "I slipped on the ice. It's a wee sprain. Nothin too serious."

The man dismounted. He strolled toward her with long confident strides. "Allow me to assist you home?"

Carstine shook her head. She wasn't foolish enough to mount a horse with a strange man. Certainly not in a country she wasn't familiar with. "I haven't far tae go. Fox Grove Hall is just around the bend. I can see myself there," Carstine said.

"Nonsense," he insisted, then met her gaze with a confident smile. "Blake Fox, Earl of Edgemore at your service." He gave a sweeping bow. "You must be Lady Minerva's new maid?"

Carstine narrowed her eyes on him. The man did bear a striking resemblance to Lady Minerva. His coloring was fairer, but the almond shape of his eyes and high cheekbones were precisely the same. She cleared her throat. "It's a pleasure to meet ye, my lord, though I fear ye are mistaken about Lady Minerva."

"Nonsense." He waved his hand. "My sister would have my hide if I left her maid out in the snow, and injured at that. Come along." He reached his hand out to her.

Maid? The word echoed in her mind, and Carstine narrowed her eyes. Whatever would make him think she was a servant? She glanced down at her wet skirt and muddied boots. She may be a bit disheveled, but she was no maid.

"Don't be stubborn." Lord Edgemore wiggled his fingers impatiently. "Come, I'll help you onto the horse."

"Nae." Carstine shook her head. "I'll not be ridin with ye."

"But of course you will. You are in my sister's employment and, therefore, my responsibility." He took a step closer, the crisp breeze stirring the golden locks that hung near his shoulders. "I know you Scots are used to the cold, but you'll freeze if you stay out much longer." He captured her arm and nudged her to stand. "Don't be stubborn."

Carstine's cheeks flamed with angry heat. She

jerked away, then pushed to her feet. "I told ye already. It's nothin. Yer assistance is not needed."

He'd insulted her, and she could not help but be upset. And what did being Scottish have to do with anything? Did he think her to be less than him because of her heritage? Is that why he instantly decided she was a servant?

It was on the tip of Carstine's tongue to correct his misguided beliefs. However, the thought of watching his smugness crumble once they were properly introduced proved too tempting, and she swallowed back her words.

He deserved his comeuppance and the embarrassment that was sure to follow. What's more, she would delight in every uncomfortable moment he suffered. A smile stretched her lips as she imagined the look that would no doubt overtake his handsome face.

She was a wicked lass, indeed.

Carstine squealed as the earl lifted her off her feet and swung her onto his saddle. She glared at him, her chin notched defiantly. "I'll not be ridin with ye." She began lowering herself from the horses back, sliding toward the edge of the saddle. "Ye canna force me."

Lord Edgemore reached up, gripping her waist

and holding her in place. "I dare say I do not understand your objection. Nor do I care. I'll not leave you here to freeze, nor will I allow you to further your injury by walking on that ankle." He spared a glance at her boot. "You will ride."

"Nae—"

"That is an order." He pushed her more firmly onto the saddle. "And I warn you now; I'll brook no further argument."

Carstine huffed an irritated sigh. "Then ye will guide the horse," she tossed the reins down at him. "As ye walk."

Satisfaction flooded her as Lord Edgemore took the reins and began leading the horse toward Fox Grove Hall. The highhanded, smug lord may have insulted her, but at least in this, she'd gotten the best of him. The knowledge that there was more to come vastly improved her mood.

Carstine turned her attention to the countryside as she relaxed in the saddle. She would soon have the full measure of her revenge.

Get Your Copy

Amanda Mariel, an accomplished wordsmith, holds dual master's degrees in liberal arts and education, specializing in the captivating realms of history and literature. Beyond her academic pursuits, she embraces the joyful chaos of motherhood, tending to both her cherished teenagers and her trio of adored fur babies. Among them, a noble Bernese Mountain Dog named Blaze, and two cats of distinct character, Ezra and Puff, share their home.

A USA Today Bestselling luminary, Amanda Mariel conjures vivid tapestries of eras long past, drawing inspiration from the languid cadence of days gone by. With pen poised and imagination unfurled, she traverses the annals of time, weaving tales that illuminate historical landscapes with finesse and flair. Her creative spirit finds respite in reading, traversing new horizons through travel, and capturing moments through the lenses of both her camera and artistic endeavors. Yet, it is in the embrace of family that she finds her truest sanctuary.

To delve deeper into Amanda's captivating world visit www.amandamariel.com. While there, an invitation to join her newsletter promises a gateway to the latest from Amanda Mariel's literary treasury, and an opportunity to claim a complimentary eBook.

Amanda's passion extends to her readers, welcoming their voices and stories into her narrative realm. Engage with her through email at amanda@amandamariel.com, or connect via her social Media channels.

Facebook: facebook.com/AuthorAmandaMariel
Twitter: twitter.com/AmandaMarieAuth
BookBub: bookbub.com/authors/amanda-mariel
Instagram: instagram.com/authoramandamariel
TicTok: tiktoc.com/@amandamarielromance

Amidst the prose and parchment, Amanda Mariel etches a profound connection, bridging eras, hearts, and minds, creating a legacy that resonates through the corridors of time.

Ladies and Scoundrels series

Scandalous Endeavors

Scandalous Intentions

Scandalous Redemption

Scandalous Wallflower

Scandalous Liaison

Dancing with Serendipity

Fabled Love Series

Enchanted by the Earl

Captivated by the Captain

Enticed by Lady Elianna

Delighted by the Duke

Lady Archer's Creed series

Amanda Mariel writing with Christina McKnight

Theodora

Georgina

Adeline

Josephine

<u>A Wallflower's Christmas Kiss</u> (Dawn Brower)

<u>Stealing a Rogue's Kiss</u> (Amanda Mariel)

<u>Scandalized by a Rogue's Kiss</u> (Amanda Mariel)

<u>A Gypsy's Christmas kiss</u> (Dawn Brower)

<u>A Vixen's Christmas kiss</u> (Dawn Brower)

<u>Standalone titles</u>

<u>One Moonlit Tryst</u>

<u>One Enchanting Kiss</u>

<u>Christmas in the Duke's Embrace</u>

<u>One Wicked Christmas</u>

<u>A Lyon in Her Bed</u> (The Lyon's Den connected world)

<u>Courting Temptation</u> (House of Devon connected world)

<u>Forever My Rogue</u> (Love Be a Lady's Charm Connected World)

Box sets and anthologies

Visit <u>www.amandamariel.com</u> to see Amanda's current offerings.

Thank you so much for taking the time to read *Earl of Grayson*.

Your opinion matters!

Please take a moment to review this book on your favorite review site and share your opinion with fellow readers.

USA Today bestselling author

~Heartwarming historical romances that leave you breathless~

CHAPTER 1

June 1817
Bedfordshire, England

Emma Thorne's maid was dead. It was obvious based on the awkward angle of her neck, in the trail of blood drawing a vivid line down her chin and the pool of it welling from underneath her.

Emma remained at the young woman's side, holding the still-warm body. Shock had kept her scream silent thus far, but the pressure of its insistence blossomed in the back of her throat. A hand clapped over her mouth and her scream fled on a gasp.

Emma's uncle had asked her to replace a book on the shelf in the library as she'd left the room. Jenny, her lady's maid, had offered to do it as she was off on her way to visit her parents in the village. The offer of kindness had been the young woman's demise.

"Don't make a sound, my lady." A familiar male voice murmured in Emma's ear.

She tried to swing around, to meet the eyes of Hammonds, the butler she'd known for the whole of her life, for what could possess him to tell her to keep from screaming?

"Blink to show you understand what I'm telling you," he said in a low voice. "It's a matter of life and death, you see."

Emma blinked and his hand came away.

"Come to the kitchen." He stood with a furtive glimpse into the hall. "With haste, my lady." He softened his tone. "If you please."

"And leave her here?" Emma whispered in horror.

Hammonds grimaced and nodded.

Emma hesitated, her fingers curled in the damp

fabric of her maid's gown. It was of a pretty sprigged muslin Emma had given to her the prior year.

"Do you not notice she looks similar to you?" Hammonds asked.

True, the maid wore the frock once belonging to Emma and her brown hair had been twisted into a series of braids at the nape of her neck, the same way Emma often wore hers. A terrifying jolt of ice-cold fear shot down Emma's spine.

She drew away in horror, releasing the maid and allowing Hammonds to help her to her feet. Blood streaked brilliant red down the front of her gown. Jenny's blood.

Oh God, Jenny.

Hammonds pulled at Emma with surprisingly strong arms, hauling her to the kitchen. "Your uncle," he said. "He's been unhappy with your decision not to wed his son. As he's become more insistent, you've been more resistant."

Emma's brain worked to process what she'd seen, what Hammonds was saying, what it all meant. The cloying odor of gore clung in her nose, metallic with fear and death.

Hammonds thrust her into the warmth of the kitchen. The cook looked up sharply, his hands buried in a ball of dough.

"Already?" Monsieur Dubois drew his hands free and wiped the excess flour onto the front of his apron.

"Jenny is dead." Hammonds released his hold on Emma and raced across the large room to a series of pots stacked neatly against a back wall.

Dubois uttered a curse and moved around the table. He stopped short and went wide-eyed with horror at Emma's gown.

"What happened?" he demanded.

"She fell from the ladder in the library." Emma twisted the delicate emerald and pearl bracelet around her wrist, the one that had belonged to her mother before her death nearly two decades prior. "She's dead." Her voice clogged with emotion and tears burned in her eyes.

The Frenchman loosed a fresh string of curses.

"Cease your blasphemy and be useful," Hammonds said in an uncharacteristically impatient tone. "It will not be long until they discover the body is not that of Miss Emma."

The butler pushed a velvet bag into her hands. "Take this and leave. Go as far from here as you can and do not return for another month."

In a month, she would be five-and-twenty, of age to no longer require the guardianship of her uncle.

The wealthy life to which he'd grown accustomed when her father died not long after her twentieth birthday would cease. She'd refused to marry her cousin, his son. Apparently, he had devised other means to secure her wealth.

The bright streak of crimson on her gown called her attention once more. He had meant to kill her, only he'd taken Jenny's life by accident instead.

"Take this as well." Dubois thrust a misshapen sack into her free hand. A knot at the top secured the contents within. "In case you need food. It will last a few days if you use it sparingly."

"And this?" she asked, regarding the velvet bag.

"It is the money we have been able to save for you." Hammonds lowered his head reverently. "And includes our own personal savings."

She shook her head, not understanding and certainly not willing to accept. Before she could refuse, Hammonds set a hand over hers, securing the bag in her palm.

"Miss Emma, we would pay that amount a thousand times over to ensure your safety." Hammonds cast her a beseeching expression. "Please take it. Stay safe for the next month and—"

"Hammonds," a voice from somewhere in the home bellowed with rage.

Emma started at the sound, her nerves on high alert as much as they were raw with emotion - with loss, with love, with fear.

"Get you gone and Godspeed, Miss." Hammonds bowed low and left, taking time to carefully close the door.

"You must go." Dubois gently pushed her in the direction of the servants' entrance at the rear of the kitchen. "To the stables, away from here."

The heavy fall of boots on the carpeted ground came from outside the kitchen within the house.

"Now," he hissed and shoved her outside.

Emma stood, dazed by the radiant sunlight and by the whirl of what had transpired. She gritted her teeth. They had sacrificed everything for her.

It was that thought which spurred her and made her run to the stables, as Dubois had suggested.

She ran on legs she could not feel, legs which did not seem strong enough to support her. And yet they carried her to the elegant row of stables along the rear of the property.

While chaos reigned in the house, the stable was impossibly silent and still. Emma's ragged breath rasped from her throat, loud in the quiet.

The stable boy was not about, and for that she was glad. She would not want more of her servants implicated. Not after what they'd already done to aid her. Surely what they had done put them in considerable danger. The very notion gave her pause. She slipped the purse into her pocket.

"Let's see if her horse is in the stall." Conrad's deep voice came from outside, indicating her cousin was merely several feet away. "If she was on her horse, she'll be much farther."

Her heart plunged into her stomach. Fear dictated her actions, propelling her into Honey's stall, forcing her to climb upon the horse's blonde bare back. She pressed the bag of food between her stomach and the horse's large body as she leaned forward and hissed her command in Honey's ear.

They burst from the stable at a powerful speed, practically knocking over the lanky form of Conrad and her uncle.

Conrad pointed dumbly at her. "There she is."

If they said more, their words were lost in the pounding of Honey's hooves upon the dirt-packed earth and the slamming of Emma's heartbeat. They would chase her though - of that she was certain. And their horses were significantly faster.

Blast.

She bounced about Honey's back, her hands lost in the grip of her horse's white mane as she held on for dear life. The bag of food jostled free and disappeared from Honey's back. Were Emma not about to suffer to the same fate, she might have tried to grab for rough sack as it fell away. As it was, she could scarcely maintain her desperate hold. Even still, she knew without a shadow of a doubt, she would not be able to ride in this manner for long.

Rather than direct Honey to the village nearly two miles away, she steered her horse in the direction of a nearby manor, one often rented out for house parties. If it were empty, as she hoped it might be, she could use it as a place to hide, to decide her next move before her uncle and Conrad could find her.

She neared the large yellow house with its dark green shutters, and her heart fell. Several people milled about with their horses. Clearly, the manor had been rented out.

She slowed her horse, weighing her options. If only her pulse could slow as readily as her steed. As it was, her heart galloped with such power, it threatened to choke her.

She did a quick survey behind her and gave a cry of despair. There in the distance were two riders racing toward her.

She jerked Honey to a stop and leapt from the

horse, running with blind speed in the direction of the massive house. The sack of coins in her pocket thwacked and bounced brutally against her thigh, but she paid it no mind. It was of slight consequence considering the threat of danger.

Those renting the property would most surely find Honey and see her well cared for. If Emma was lucky, her uncle would assume she'd fallen off the horse's glossy back and had become lost in the foliage between the two massive manors.

Emma peered about, confirming no one had seen her, and reached for a window. It clicked under her hand, locked. In fact, all the windows and doors had been bolted tight. She gave a dejected cry and darted off to the one place she might find refuge - the stable.

~

The house party be damned. If Alistair did not go to Scotland to aid Madge in her botched whisky smuggling venture, they both might end up dead. Her, skewered through by some brigand's sword and him dangling from a rope.

It was a recklessly precarious situation requiring

immediate action on his part, especially considering the time it had taken the missive to reach him. Cold fear fissured through him. He could only rush as quickly as he could and hope he was not too late.

He strolled from the manor the Wicked Earls had rented and made his way to the stables to tell the lad there to ready the horses and a carriage. Surely there was some servant to do the task for Alistair, but he wasn't much in the mood to wait when he could bloody well do it himself.

Beast trotted along beside him, ignorant to the irritation plaguing his master if the happy loll of his pink tongue were any indication. In truth, the dog was anything but a beast. A fluffy blond bit of a thing that came to Alistair's shins no matter how much he fed him. And the creature was perpetually happy with his large brown eyes and panting smiles.

"Do you presume the old witch did it on purpose?" Alistair asked the dog.

Beast's ears perked up and he cocked his head to the side, as if in ponderous contemplation before his mouth hung open in a grin and the tongue unfurled out once more.

"That's what I thought," Alistair muttered and resumed his trek through the neatly trimmed grass to where the stables awaited. The dog loved everyone. Even Madge.

Alistair was more cynical. He wouldn't put it past his mother to intentionally do it in order to see him home once more. Before he got too "English," no doubt.

But to make a deal with one of the most notoriously foul vendors in London, and for twenty barrels – it was unheard of. Certainly Alistair had never bothered to attempt such a feat before, let alone it being something his mother could ever successfully complete.

Alistair stepped inside the stables. It was quiet within. "Are you here, lad?"

No one answered.

Beast scampered around Alistair with an excitable curiosity to explore and disappeared into an open stall.

"I say, are you here, lad?" Alistair asked again with a rough and frustrated edge.

Again no one answered.

Where were the damn servants? None were readily nearby inside the manor, and the stable lad also appeared to be absent. Since the English had the lot of them doing every last action for them save wiping their arses, shouldn't there always be someone about?

A horse stamped its hoof and whinnied.

Damn, but it was frustrating having to stop his life in England and rush home to see to his mother's affairs. If she couldn't manage the whisky business on her own, he'd demand she stop. He could not keep on with it, constantly getting her out of these situations she seemed to find herself implicated in.

At least the others had been easily managed from London.

He shuddered to think what might happen to her if he were unable to ease her troubles, especially when her predicaments were the direct result of profligate practices. His mother needed no money. He saw to it she was well cared for and funds delivered to perpetuate the restorations at Lochslin.

"Did ye require me, m'lord?" MacKenzie, Alistair's valet and longtime friend, appeared in the stables.

"I cannot find the stable lad," Alistair said irritably. "We must get back to Scotland posthaste."

"Is this an urgent matter, or will we be leaving by the end of the week after the party has ended?" MacKenzie leveled his dark eyes at Alistair, efficient at understanding the situation by this point. After all, he'd been Alistair's valet for the better part of a year – the entirety of Alistair's inherited earldom.

Alistair dragged a hand through his shoulder-length hair. The length of it was a concession the ton was willing to overlook in light of his influential wealth. It was incredible the things one might get away with when they were enormously rich. Certainly several of the ladies had mentioned the appeal of his longer hair and the wildness it lent him, especially when paired with his kilt. And only his kilt.

"Madge is making trouble again." Alistair did a surreptitious scan around the stables, confirming the stable lad was not within earshot. Nevertheless, he spoke in the code they'd used when they'd smuggled whisky together, on the off chance someone might be nearby. "She made a deal for twenty portions."

"Twenty?" MacKenzie balked.

"My sentiments exactly."

MacKenzie lowered his head and pursed his lips under his well-trimmed black beard. "Ye canna get caught."

"Nor can I leave her to fend for herself."

The wide window at the front wall revealed several riders approaching in the distance.

"Ready the trunks for departure." Alistair did not take his eyes off the riders. "We leave within the hour."

MacKenzie nodded and left the stables to do as he was bid, as always without complaint or protest. A good loyal Scot.

A high-pitched whine came from the open stall.

"Beast," Alistair called. "Come."

As this call typically resulted in the bounding form of the overly joyous creature, Beast's lack of compliance gave Alistair pause.

"Beast." He peered into the stall and found the dog sitting beside a mound of hay, which he watched with serious intensity.

Beast barked at the pile and pawed at the loosening bits along the outer edges. A white stocking encasing a neat ankle became visible. As soon as it was seen, it snapped out of sight once more.

"What the devil?" Alistair carefully swept aside the straw to reveal a woman blinking up at him.

Stalks of hay jutted from the tousled brown hair which fell wild about her face. She stared at him with narrowed blue eyes and a stubborn set to her brows. Her mouth wore none of her defiance, however. No, it was lush and red and vulnerable.

There were women at the house to be sure, but not ladies with creamy white skin wearing gowns of fine muslin. And certainly none with a note of fear in their eyes.

Alistair startled at her appearance. "Have you been hurt?"

The riders stopped outside the front of the stables and leapt from the horses. The woman slinked deeper into the pile of hay, rounding her shoulders as if she might be able to make herself disappear.

Beast issued forth a low growl. Alistair cocked a brow at the dog who had never once made a sound of displeasure in his newly happy life.

Before he could ask either the girl for her grievances, or bother understanding the dog, the heavy footfall of boots came from the entrance to the stables. It was not the stable lad who entered, of course, but an elderly gentleman and a tall man with fair hair and an arrogant lift to his chin.

"Forgive the intrusion," the older man said with an amiable smile. "I understand you are renting this manor, and I do not mean to intrude upon your house party. I do, however, require your assistance."

"Do you?" Alistair asked with the bored disinterest of the cultured elite.

The man surveyed the area with an open rudeness that set Alistair on edge. "Evans is the name. You see, I'm searching for my niece. It appears she has run away and was last seen near here. I hoped you might help me in finding her."

Download Today

PROLOGUE

May 1816
London, England

London was dismally gray with rain the day Alistair Johnstone attempted to decline his inherited earldom. It did little good for him to bother, he knew, save for Madge's sake. Yet, try he did, and had been promptly met with the unamused blinking of the solicitor. Dejected and titled, Alistair gazed out the window where puddles of mud reflected a gray sky. A dog with jutting bones rummaged with desperation and skittishness through the rubbish piled in the alleyway.

Madge always did have poor taste in lodgings.

The door slammed closed. She had returned, and yet he was not ready to face her. Outside, the miserable creature drew a piece of waste and hunkered over the prize in a protective gesture.

"Well, how did it go with the solicitor? What was it all about?" Madge's thick Scottish burr cut through the intensely silent room.

"My grandfather has passed on." Alistair continued to watch the poor beast.

Madge scoffed. "Good riddance to that bastard. Were it no' for him, yer da and I could've been happy. He put us against one another."

Alistair bit back a long-suffering sigh. He didn't want to hear the story of it again, not today. "I've inherited his earldom."

Madge coughed out a wheezing laugh. Finally, Alistair put his back to the window and faced his mother. Though age and hard years had left her face creased, her hair was the same shade of luminous red that had caught his father's eye. Her cheeks were flushed with mirth and her blue eyes sparkled with it. "Ye canna be serious." The smile wilted somewhat and she straightened her skinny frame. "Well, ye said no, aye?"

"I did. But as anticipated, I have no choice." Alistair steeled himself between the clash of his own blood which ran in equal parts English and Scottish and said the truth of it for the first time since he'd spoken with the solicitor late that morning. "I am now the Earl of Benton."

The blue of his mother's eyes went sharp with reproach. "One can always say no."

"This is not one of those instances." Alistair folded his hands behind his back and resisted the urge to let his attention go to the window once more. "Were I to say no, I would face the wrath of the king."

"An English king," Madge hissed. "I dinna care a fat toad what the English king wants."

"This will be of great benefit to you," Alistair continued, intentionally ignoring her treasonous remark. Time had taught him reprimands for such things fell on deaf ears with Madge. "It affords us the opportunity to repair Lochslin Castle, which sorely requires a great many things. Whisky smuggling doesn't provide nearly enough—"

"The whisky smuggling." Madge snapped upright. "Ye'll still be doing it, aye?"

Somewhere down the hall, another inhabitant of

the rickety inn slammed a door and stomped away. If only Alistair could be so lucky as to readily escape. Instead he drew a deep breath in the hopes of bringing in some patience with it.

"I cannot run whisky any longer, Madge. It is considered treason."

"By the bloody English king," she muttered.

"And I could lose my life for it."

"So ye'll give up one of yer grandda's legacy for the other?" Her lips puckered as if she had something bitter lodged in her mouth. "Yer Scottish ancestry for yer English."

The final threads of Alistair's tolerance were shredding under his mother's insistent refusal to listen. "I do not have a choice," he said through clenched teeth.

"We'll see what can be done when we get back to Scotland." Madge stopped speaking abruptly and slowly angled her face to Alistair. "Ye will be coming home to Scotland, aye?" Her tone was softer, hesitant. If he didn't know Madge so well, he might have even assumed she was frightened.

His chest drew tight. For all Madge's prickly exterior, within she was a fierce mother set on protecting her only child. And what he would say next might possibly break her heart.

"I will not be going to Scotland."

The proud stance Madge had displayed crumpled. "The bastard has won," she whispered. "He tried to steal ye from me when ye were but a lad. I insisted ye come home despite yer da's protest because he dinna see it. He dinna see it. But I did. That English whoreson meant to take ye from me, to sway ye to yer English side. And now he's won."

Alistair inwardly cringed at her words. His grandfather had wanted what was best for him. In truth, those years at Eton had afforded him friendships he would have never been able to find in the wilds of Scotland at Lochslin Castle. Those would be integral in his assuming the earldom smoothly and entering the ton. "It was not a battle, Madge. He—"

"He made ye full English is what he did." She waved a bony hand at him. "Look at ye, with yer fine English coat and yer crisp speech and yer unaffected demeanor. And in an instant ye're an English earl, living on English soil." She sniffled. "Ye're lost to me, son. I've lost ye."

Alistair handed his mother his handkerchief, which she deftly pushed away. "Madge, I am still Scottish." He gestured to his kilt with exasperation. "I proudly wear the Munro colors. I will eventually be home to assist you in overseeing the repairs to

Lochslin and ensure you are well." Outside the window, a small group of urchins circled rage dog. The creature had curled in on itself with its tail tucked between its legs.

"Leave me," Madge said with wounded vehemence. "I'll smuggle the whisky without ye. I'll repair Lochslin without ye. I'll live my life without ye."

Alistair twisted from the window, pulled by the weight of his heavy heart. "Madge, I—"

A vase flew past his head and slammed into the wall where it shattered. Alistair jerked to the side as another article hurtled toward his face, narrowly avoiding being struck.

"Leave me." Madge snatched up a metal cup from the bedside table and drew it back.

Alistair knew too well how her tantrums went and strode across the room at a clipped pace. He opened the door and paused. "I'll always be your son, Madge."

He didn't know what made him say it. Some deep childhood memory for the woman who would rock him in her arms when he had night terrors, and had fought for him with the force of a lion. He was aware that in her own twisted way, this rage was driven by the fear of losing him. Madge never did deal well with hurt.

Perhaps that was why he'd taken the time to say it, risking the integrity of his face as the cup came hurtling through the air at him. He closed the door in time for the weight of the projectile to thunk solidly against it.

A scream sounded from the other side, wild and raw. It tore into his heart, but there was no reasoning with Madge. Not when she was like this. He treaded down the narrow stairs, ignoring the wobbling banister which had more possibility of upsetting one's balance than solidifying it, and remembered the dog.

He quickened his pace and exited the building to find the boys tossing rocks in the direction of the beast. It did not snarl and snap at them as others might have done. No, it merely cringed deeper into itself as if attempting to make itself disappear. Alistair was well acquainted with that feeling, one of wishing to simply become invisible.

"Get on with you," Alistair said in a low, warning tone. "Leave the creature be."

A boy with a mop of shaggy brown hair surveyed Alistair up and down. "We'll do what we want." He sneered, revealing a missing front tooth, and lobbed a stone at Alistair. The bit of rock sank into the mud at Alistair's feet.

"I said get on with ye," he snarled, the Scottish burr of his youth thickening his accent in his rage. For it was not only the boy who he was angry with, it was the injustice of the starving beast, the cowardice of children pitching stones at a defenseless animal, and it was Madge and her damned stubbornness.

The boys scowled and ran from him, scattering in multiple directions like vermin. A soft whimpering rose came from the ground and a pair of liquid brown eyes gazed imploringly up at Alistair.

He reached down and patted the dog's wet, matted head. The beast nestled closer to him, desperate for affection. Alistair looked up the front of the inn to Madge's window where all had gone quiet.

At least with the beast at his side, he could help. Madge was too obstinate to listen to reason.

"Come on, then." He made his way down the muddy street to the better part of town. A glance confirmed the dog had not moved. Alistair whistled and the creature cocked his head, the pink of its tongue protruding from the side of its mouth.

"Come on," Alistair repeated and waved his hand.

This time the beast did not hesitate. It sprinted to him at full tilt, its muddy brown ears flapping about its head. And together, the two of them, neither one cut from the fine cloth of London society, made their way into a world that would otherwise have cast them readily aside.

www.ingramcontent.com/pod-product-compliance
Lightning Source LLC
Chambersburg PA
CBHW071439130726
47997CB00006B/2151